CLOSE
TO THE
BONE

CLOSE
TO THE
BONE

WILLIAM G. TAPPLY

St. Martin's Press
New York

A THOMAS DUNNE BOOK.
An imprint of St. Martin's Press.

Design by Nancy Resnick

Library of Congress Cataloging-in-Publication Data

Tapply, William G.
    Close to the bone / by William G. Tapply. —1st ed.
      p.   cm.
    "A Thomas Dunne book."
    ISBN 0–312–14567–5
    1. Coyne, Brady (Fictitious character)—Fiction. 2. Lawyers—
Massachusetts—Boston—Fiction. 3. Boston (Mass.)—Fiction.
I. Title.
PS3570.A568C59   1996
813'.54—dc20   96–18990
                                            CIP

First Edition: September 1996

10 9 8 7 6 5 4 3 2 1

for Vicki

who's on every page
with thanks
and love

Justice, though due to the accused, is due to the accuser also.

—Benjamin Cardozo

I went to the woods because I wished to live deliberately, to front only the essential facts of life, and see if I could not learn what it had to teach, and not, when I came to die, discover that I had not lived. I did not wish to live what was not life, living is so dear; nor did I wish to practise resignation, unless it was quite necessary. I wanted to live deep and suck out all the marrow of life, to live so sturdily and Spartanlike as to put to rout all that was not life, to cut a broad swath and shave close, to drive life into a corner, and reduce it to its lowest terms, and, if it proved to be mean, why then to get the whole and genuine meanness of it, and publish its meanness to the world; or if it were sublime, to know it by experience, and be able to give a true account of it in my next excursion.

—Henry David Thoreau

ACKNOWLEDGMENTS

I am indebted to Vicki Stiefel, Rick Boyer, Jed Mattes, and Elisabeth Story for their perceptive help on this yarn. My heartfelt thanks.

CLOSE
TO THE
BONE

1

Julie keeps telling me I'll never be a proper lawyer if I keep driving out to the suburbs to meet my clients at their homes whenever they request it. The clients, she maintains, are supposed to come to the lawyer's office in the city. They should make appointments, preferably weeks ahead of time because, according to Julie, any lawyer who can see a client at a moment's notice can't be very busy, and if he's not very busy he can't be much good, and if he's not much good then clients will not be inclined to make appointments with him in the first place. When it's done properly, says Julie, the clients who appear in their lawyer's office at their appointed time should be kept waiting while the lawyer accrues billable hours with another client, who has also been kept waiting.

Julie is probably a better legal secretary than I am a lawyer. I know that if I listened to her I'd accrue more billable hours, which is how Julie measures the success of a law practice.

So when Roger Falconer called on a gray Tuesday afternoon in November and said he needed to confer with me immediately, I said, "I've got an opening at four-thirty, Roger," as Julie had trained me to do.

My heart wasn't in it, of course. Roger Falconer, I knew, simply didn't sit in the waiting rooms of lawyers or doctors—or governors or senators or the CEOs of multinational corporations, either.

Hell, Roger Falconer had *been* the CEO of a multinational corporation before he retired. Back in the sixties and early seventies he had also been the state attorney general and the Republican candidate for governor and, apparently encouraged by losing that one, for United States senator. He lost that election, too, but, as he liked to point out, what could a Republican expect in Massachusetts, the only state that failed to cast its electoral votes for Nixon in 1972?

In fact, a lot of people who courted Roger's influence or money, or both, still called him "Senator," and he didn't bother to correct them.

I called him Roger. He didn't try to correct me, either.

"Four-thirty, huh?" he said. "Your last appointment of the day?"

"Uh huh." I knew what was coming, and I was helpless to avoid it.

"You should be able to be here by five-thirty, then," he said.

I sighed. "Sure, Roger. I guess I can be there around five-thirty. What's up?"

"A matter of utmost gravity, I'm afraid. I'd rather not discuss it over the phone, Brady."

When I slipped into my trench coat and headed out of the office a few minutes after four-thirty, Julie arched her eyebrows from behind her computer monitor.

"I'm off to see Roger Falconer," I said. "I've got to be there at five-thirty, and I don't need any shit about which of us is the mountain and which is Mahomet. It's a matter of utmost gravity."

"I didn't say anything," she said.

"Yeah, but I know what you're thinking."

She flashed her pretty blue-eyed Irish smile. "Utmost gravity? Did you actually say that?"

"Roger's words."

"Hey," she said with an elaborate shrug. "It's your law practice. If you want to go traipsing around the countryside at the summons of doddering old political has-beens, why should I care?"

"You should care, of course. That's your job. And I'm glad I've got you to do it."

"I don't see why the old poop can't come to the office like everyone else."

"Well, he won't. If I didn't go to him, he'd just get himself another lawyer." I bent and kissed her cheek. "I'll fill you in tomorrow."

It took over an hour to negotiate the rush-hour traffic from Copley Square, out Storrow Drive onto Route 2 and thence to Lincoln. I turned onto Route 126—Thoreau had called it "the Walden road"—and drove past the pond and the acres of fields and forests that the Lincoln town fathers and mothers have preserved from development so that folks like Roger Falconer can live thoroughly insulated from the riffraff.

Roger's long driveway wound through the dark oak and pine woods, past the tennis court and the swimming pool and the putting green, and ended in a turnaround in front of his big, square Federal-period colonial. Floodlights mounted under the eaves lit the flower gardens and the lawn, now mostly frost-killed and brown and littered with dead leaves. Orange lights glowed from every window.

A little white two-seater Mercedes convertible was parked behind a gunmetal gray Range Rover. I pulled in at the end of the line and got out of my car. A northeast wind hissed through the pine trees and rattled the clumps of dried leaves in the oaks. It felt damp and chilly on my face. It would bring freezing rain or wet snow. In November it could go either way. I climbed the front steps and rang the bell. A minute later the door swung open and a youngish woman I didn't recognize greeted me with a frown.

She wore a dark blue wool dress with a high neck and a low hem, just a touch of eye shadow and lip gloss, and no jewelry except for a diamond the size of a Brazil nut on her left hand, the hand that was holding a can of Coke. A slim blonde, pretty in a cool, brittle, elegantly fashionable way, early thirties, I guessed. "You are . . . ?" she said.

"Brady Coyne," I said. "I have an appointment with Roger. And you?"

"Pardon?"

"We haven't met," I said.

"I'm sorry." She tried on a smile that didn't quite make it up to her eyes. "Brenda Falconer. I'm the Senator's daughter-in-law." She lifted her Coke and took a quick, nervous sip.

"Glen's wife?" I said.

"Yes." She smiled again, and it worked better this time. "That, too." She extended her hand and allowed me to touch it for a moment. Then she turned. "They're in the library," she said over her shoulder. "This way."

I followed her down the wide center hallway and through a living room full of clunky old antique furniture and decorated with dark portraits of clunky old men. We stopped outside the open doorway to Roger's library, which was a room as big as my entire apartment. At the far end a brace of golden retrievers—Abe and Ike, named after Roger's political heroes—slept on the hearth by a blazing fieldstone fireplace. The walls were lined floor to ceiling with old leather-bound volumes. Rolltop desks and oak tables and leather sofas and armchairs were scattered about, and seated in two of the armchairs were Roger Falconer and his son, Glen. They were studying the fire, apparently ignoring each other.

Brenda cleared her throat and the two men looked up. "Ah, Brady," said Roger. "Come, sit. Brenda, dear, get Brady a drink."

"I can get my own drink," I said to her.

She shook her head. "It's okay. Really. What would you like?"

"I'll have what you're having," I said to her. "Thanks."

She left the room and I went over to where Roger and Glen were sitting. Empty highball glasses rested on the table between them. Roger didn't bother rising as we shook hands. He was almost completely bald now, and I knew he was closing in on eighty, but he still could've passed for the man who had run for the Senate back in the early seventies. His pale eyes glittered with enthusiasm and conspiracy, and his grip was strong. "You remember Glen?" he said.

"Sure." I held out my hand to the younger man. "How are you?"

4

"Not that good, actually," Glen said. He stood to shake hands with me. He was several inches taller than my six feet, and his face was longer and more angular than his father's. His sandy hair had receded perceptibly since the last time I had seen him, which had been a few years earlier.

After we sat down, Glen leaned toward me. "Look—"

"Brady," interrupted Roger, "we have a problem."

"I figured," I said. "A matter of utmost gravity, I think you called it. Sounds like a problem to me."

"A week and a half ago," he said, "Glen had an automobile accident. He, um, there was a collision with another vehicle."

"Who hit whom?" I said, addressing my question to Glen.

But it was Roger who answered. "He hit them."

"Them?"

"There were two passengers in the other car," said Roger. "A woman and her four-year-old boy."

He paused, gazing at me with his eyebrows arched behind his steel-rimmed glasses, waiting for me to figure it out. I did, but I said nothing.

There was a discreet rap at the door, and then Brenda came in. She handed me a glass of Coke rattling with ice cubes. I looked up at her. "Thanks," I said.

She nodded. "You're welcome." She stood there, looking from Roger to Glen.

"Thank you, my dear," said Roger with a nod, dismissing her.

Her eyes flickered and met mine for a moment before she turned and left the room. The door latched softly behind her.

"Your wife isn't included in this matter, huh?" I said to Glen.

"Family business," said Roger, who apparently did not consider wives to be members of his family.

I shrugged and took a sip of Coke.

"The woman was seriously injured in the collision," Roger said. He cleared his throat. "She died this morning."

"Right," I said. "And Glen was drunk."

Roger nodded.

"And they're going to charge him."

"Yes. Vehicular homicide, DUI."

"What about the little boy?"

"He was in a car seat. He's okay."

"Lucky," I said.

Roger nodded. "I guess so."

"I don't do these kinds of cases," I said.

"I know," said Roger. "But you're my lawyer."

"Did you take a Breathalyzer?" I said to Glen.

He nodded. "I flunked. My license was suspended."

"But you weren't charged?"

"No. Not then." He glanced at his father.

"I took care of it," said Roger. "But now, with the woman, ah, failing to survive . . ."

"You can't take care of this," I said.

Roger shook his head. "We need a good lawyer."

"You need a miracle."

Glen leaned toward me. "Listen, Brady—"

"Shut up," said Roger conversationally. "Brady's right, and if it weren't our family's name that the newspapers will be plastering all over the front page, I'd leave you out there twisting in the wind." He turned to me. "Do you know any miracle workers?"

"Yes, as a matter of fact."

"Who?"

"I'll talk to him."

"I'd rather—"

"Do you want me to handle it, Roger?"

"I do."

"Good. I will handle it." I drained my Coke and stood up. "That's it, then. I'll be in touch with you."

Roger looked up at me. "Brady," he said, "it's—"

"I know. A matter of utmost gravity. I'll call you tomorrow."

He pushed himself out of his chair. Glen started to stand, but Roger said, "I'll see Brady out," and Glen sat down again.

I held out my hand to Glen. "Good luck," I said.

He shrugged and we shook. "Thanks."

Roger followed me back through the living room to the front

door. I didn't see Brenda. I put my coat on and opened the door. "He doesn't seem that contrite," I said.

"My son is an alcoholic," said Roger, as if that explained everything.

"It's hard to be sympathetic."

Roger nodded. "He's looking at prison time, isn't he?"

"Sounds like it."

"How much?"

"Not enough," I said.

2

Alexandria Shaw was waiting for me when I got to my apartment a little after seven-thirty. Her feet were bare and she was wearing a pair of my sweatpants and one of my raggedy old Yale T-shirts, and she was curled in the corner of the sofa prodding at her scalp with the business end of a pencil and frowning through her big round glasses at a yellow legal pad. My old black-and-white television was tuned to *Jeopardy,* but Alex didn't seem to be watching it.

I went over and kissed the back of her neck. "I didn't have a chance to call," I said. "I was hoping you'd be here."

"Gimme a minute, sweetie," she mumbled.

"Working on a story?"

"Mmm."

I threw my trench coat over the back of a chair, followed my nose into the kitchen, and lifted the lid off the pot that was simmering on the stove. I took a sniff, then went back into the living room. "Lentils, huh?" I said.

She looked up, poked her glasses up onto the bridge of her nose with her forefinger, and smiled. "Lentils are very good for you."

"You don't mind if I add some hot sausages, do you?"

"Hot sausages taste good," she said. "An unbeatable combination, lentils and sausages. Something that tastes good to neutralize something that's good for you. I brought garlic bread and salad stuff, too, if you want to throw it together."

In the refrigerator there were half a dozen Italian sausages that I had grilled a couple of days earlier. I cut them into bite-sized chunks and added them to Alex's lentil soup. I tossed a green salad in a wooden bowl and put the loaf of garlic bread into the oven and set it for "warm." Then I poured two fingers of Rebel Yell over a glass of ice cubes. I took the glass into the bedroom, where I climbed out of my suit and into a pair of jeans and a flannel shirt.

When I returned to the living room, Alex was sipping from a bottle of Samuel Adams lager and watching the television. I paused in the doorway and gazed at her sprawled on my sofa, dressed in my baggy old sweatpants, with a pencil stuck over her ear and her glasses slipped down toward the end of her nose. She looked incredibly sexy.

I'd met her in May. Within a few weeks we were exchanging "sleepovers," and on Labor Day weekend we'd exchanged house keys. During my entire ten years of divorced bachelorhood, I'd never done anything like that.

Oh, we kept our separate apartments—hers on Marlborough Street in Back Bay and mine in the high-rise overlooking Boston Harbor. We did not quite concede that we were living together. But that's about what it amounted to.

It should have felt strange and stressful to a man who'd been alone for a decade and had conscientiously avoided making any commitments to a woman in that time. But it didn't. With Alex, it felt natural and logical.

"Macedonia," she called out suddenly.

"*What is* Macedonia," I corrected. "You've got to give the question."

She nodded without taking her eyes from the television, and a moment later she said, "Carthage! *What is* Carthage, I mean."

I slumped onto the sofa beside her. She leaned her cheek toward me and I gave her a loud, wet kiss.

"Mmm," she said. "Nice."

"How're you doing?"

"I've gotten practically all of them right so far."

"Good. That's not what I meant."

"Oh. Like, how was my day?"

"Like that, yes."

"Turn that thing off, will you?"

"Gladly." I reached over and snapped off the television. Then I slumped back on the sofa.

Alex wiggled against me and laid her cheek on my shoulder. "Wanna start again?"

"Sure," I said. I turned, touched her hair, and kissed her softly on the lips. "How was your day?" I said.

"Good. Fine." She nuzzled my throat. "Had an interview with the governor. If you think stories about the implications of Massachusetts converting to a graduated state income tax are exciting, I had a helluva day."

"If anyone can make those stories exciting, you can," I said.

"Yes, I can," she said. "How're you?"

I blew out a long sigh. "It was okay until the end. Sometimes I feel like a goddamn glorified butler for all the self-important old farts who are my clients. I had to drive all the way out to Lincoln at four-thirty for a conversation that would've taken ten minutes on the telephone because Roger Falconer doesn't make office visits and thinks his business is too fucking grave to conduct on the telephone. 'A matter of the utmost gravity.' That's what he called it. So instead of getting home at five-thirty, it's, what, nearly eight?"

"Almost eight, yes," she said softly. "I thought you liked your clients."

I nodded. "Oh, I do. I don't accept clients I don't like. But some of them can be pretty damn self-important. Sometimes it gets to me. Whatever happened to the guy who was going to argue civil liberties cases before the Supreme Court?"

"Your career took a different turn, Brady. You do what you do, and you're very good at it, and you're your own boss, and it makes you a lot of money. There are worse things."

I sipped from my drink. "There are better things, too. I mean,

Billy's out there in Idaho, a ski instructor in the winter and a trout-fishing guide in the summer and a bartender in his spare time. I'd like to do that."

"Your son is a twenty-one-year-old college dropout," she said. "You're not."

"No," I said. "Not even close. There are times I wish I was, though. I'd like to drop out and head for the Rockies, even if I'm not twenty-one."

Her hand squeezed my leg. "Would you bring me with you?"

"Out West?"

"Yes. Would you come?"

"You bet."

"Why not do it? Let's do it, Brady."

I sighed. This was one of Alex's favorite conversational topics. "Sure."

"What's stopping you?" she persisted. "Billy's off on his own, Joey's got that scholarship to Stanford. You've fulfilled all your obligations. It's time to live your own life."

"My clients—"

"Can't get along without you. I know." She snuggled against me. "I'd do it. I really would."

"You would, huh?"

"Sure. We could buy a little ranch. We'd have horses."

"And dogs."

"Yes," she said. "Dogs. And cats, too, and maybe a goat. And a meadow for some cows, and beyond it a view of the mountains—"

"Don't forget the trout stream running through the meadow."

"Right. So I could watch you catch trout while I sat in the hot tub."

"And afterwards I'd join you in the hot tub, and we could watch the sun set and drink beer."

"Mmm," she said. "Nice. Really nice."

"Could we really do that?"

"Sure," she mumbled. "Why not?"

"What about your career?"

"You mean," she said, "what about *your* career?" She blew out a sigh. "Or maybe you mean, what about our relationship? If we did that, you'd never get rid of me."

"I don't want to get rid of you." I nuzzled the back of her neck. She looked up at me. "No?"

"No. It was nice coming home, sniffing the aroma of lentil soup, and finding you here."

"It happens a lot that way."

"And it's always nice."

"Well," she said, "I'd go out West with you. I would. Then I guess I'd be there every day, and maybe you wouldn't like that so much. You'd get sick of lentil soup."

"I *would* like it. Especially if you let me put hot sausages in it."

"But it won't happen," she said. "I understand."

I laid my head on the back of the sofa and gazed up at the ceiling. "Sometimes I think I'm turning into an old fart myself," I said.

"You're more like a middle-aged fart," she said.

"I mean," I persisted, "you're right. What's stopping me? The boys have grown wings and flown away. I've had a little career, made some money. My clients don't need me. There are certainly plenty of lawyers who can do what I do. I hate living in the city. I hate feeling I've got to jump when I get a summons from people like Roger Falconer. I could be a bartender."

"You'd make a lovely bartender," Alex said.

"Or a trout guide. I could do that."

"I bet you'd like that," she said.

I sighed. "It's fun to think about."

She sat up, turned, and frowned at me. "You're stuck, sweetie. You should try to get unstuck. Life is too short."

"I know." I pushed myself to my feet. "Let's eat."

After supper Alex and I pulled on sweatshirts and sat out on the balcony overlooking the harbor. A misty rain swirled in the wind, and whitecaps glittered in the city lights, but we were protected from most of it by the building and the balcony above us. We sipped coffee and I smoked a cigarette.

"I heard about Glen Falconer's accident," she said.

Alex is a reporter for the *Globe,* and she knows that I must protect the confidentiality of my clients. Some aspects of my business I cannot discuss with anybody, but especially not with a reporter, even if she's the woman who has a key to my apartment and makes lentil soup for me. So she never asks me questions. Some of the information she gets in her job as a reporter is confidential, too, so I don't ask her questions, either. Sometimes our conversations are elliptical, and sometimes we have to search for topics we can both talk about freely.

Sometimes we can talk elliptically and still help each other do our jobs.

"What'd you hear?" I asked her.

"He flunked the Breathalyzer. He was driving a big car and he collided with a little Honda. Two people were hurt."

"One of them died this morning," I said.

"I didn't know," she said. "Shit, I hate it when that happens."

"Me, too." We were quiet for a couple of minutes, then I said, "What else did you hear?"

"He either rolled through a stop sign or failed to look before he entered an intersection. The Honda had the right of way. He sideswiped her. She swerved into a parked car. Her chest hit the steering column."

"No seat belt?"

"I guess not. The other passenger was a child in a car seat. Not injured. So they're charging him, huh?"

"You'll probably read about it in tomorrow's *Globe,*" I said.

"Falconer's a big name in Boston."

"Roger's is."

"Glen's got lots of his daddy's money," she said. "Ergo, his is a big name, too. This isn't his first, you know."

I nodded. Glen's license had been suspended once before for DUI when he was nailed for speeding on Route 95. He had taken the class required by the Commonwealth for convicted drunk drivers, got his license back, and then apparently resumed his old ways.

"In Sweden, I think it is," I said, "one conviction and you lose your license for life."

"Sensible people, the Swedes." She reached for my hand and squeezed it. Out on the harbor a big oil tanker was inching through the chop. "I'm getting chilly," she whispered. "Almost ready for bed?"

"Definitely."

"You're not defending him, are you?"

I laughed. "Not me, babe. Glen needs a magician, not some paper pusher."

"You're not a paper pusher, Brady. You're a fine attorney."

"Hey," I said. "I am one helluva paper pusher. You want some paper pushed, see Brady Coyne. Don't knock paper pushing."

She squeezed my thigh. "I'm sorry. You are indeed a superior paper pusher, and a noble profession it is. So who're you getting to defend Glen Falconer?"

"Paul Cizek, if I can persuade him to take the case."

"Ah," she said. "The Houdini of the criminal courts."

"Paul's the closest thing to a magician I know," I said. I stood up and held both of my hands down to Alex. "Come on. I've got a magic trick I'd like to show you."

3

The next morning I left a message with Paul Cizek's secretary at Tarlin and Overton. He called me back a little before noon. "How's the mighty fisherman?" he said when Julie connected us.

"Alas," I said, "yet another season hath ended and I did not wet nearly enough lines to satisfy my lust. And you and I never did spend time together on the water."

"Too bad, too," he said. "I found stripers and blues in every creek and estuary and tidal flat on the north shore. I found them in the rips and in the surf and against the rocks and—"

"And you caught them on eels and sandworms and herring and bunker."

"Do I detect scorn in your tone, Coyne?"

"Scorn? No. I know you fish with nothing but bait. It's a pretty low-down way to do it, but you—"

"I'm a pretty low-down guy," said Paul, "not to handicap myself with flimsy fly rods and elegant little handcrafted confections of hair and feather that have no smell to them. *Chacun à son qout,* if you ask me. The fishing was pretty damn good, and you missed it. Now the boat's in the garage and my gear is stowed away for another dreary New England winter."

"Next year," I said.

"Yeah. You keep saying that."

"Just call me. I'll come."

"You willing to arise before the sun and witness the dawn of a new day from the deck of *Olivia* with me?"

"Absolutely. And how is Olivia?"

"You mean the boat or the wife?"

"The wife. I know you take good care of the boat."

"Olivia's good. Asks after you all the time. Keeps saying we should get together. Wants to meet your Alex. Olivia's been kicking some serious water-polluting ass. Her little group's got three civil suits and two criminal cases pending. She's really into it, and I admire the hell out of her. Some weeks we hardly see each other. She's off watchdogging local zoning- and planning-board hearings, testifying before legislative subcommittees, making speeches, harassing lawmakers, organizing fund-raisers, and I—"

"You, I understand, are kicking some serious butt yourself, Paul."

I heard him sigh. "I've won a few cases."

"What I hear, you've won some impossible cases."

"The presumption of innocence is a powerful ally, Brady."

"And the assembled might of the state's district attorneys makes a powerful adversary. No kidding, you've pulled some out of a hat."

"Yeah, I guess." He was silent for a moment. Then he said, "So what's up?"

"I've got a case for you."

"Tell me about it."

"You know who Roger Falconer is."

"Sure. Everybody knows Falconer. What'd he do?"

"Nothing. Or at least nothing that anyone's going to indict him for. It's his son."

"Glen's his name, right?"

"Yes. He's about to be charged with vehicular homicide."

"DUI?"

"You got it."

"Did he do it?"

"He was driving the car, all right. They got him on the Breathalyzer. The woman died yesterday."

"Aw, shit," he said.

"So what do you say?"

"I gotta check a few things. I'll get back to you this afternoon."

Paul called back around three and told me that Tarlin and Overton was inclined to accept the Falconer case, but before he made a firm commitment he wanted to meet with Glen. We agreed to assemble in my office at seven that evening.

I asked Julie to call and set it up. "Roger'll probably want to be in on it and try to talk you into holding the conference out in Lincoln. That's unacceptable. If Roger insists on joining us, fine. But it's got to be here. I want Glen in my office at seven, or else he'll have to do his own shopping for a lawyer."

Julie grinned. "I can do that."

"I know," I said. "You do it better than I do."

"You don't do it at all."

"That's because it's your job," I said.

She buzzed me five minutes later. "All set," she said. "The old man grumbled and wanted to talk to you. I told him you were tied up. They'll be here at seven."

"Both of them?"

"That is my inference, yes."

"Sure," I said. "Roger'll want a firsthand look at Paul. I don't think he lets Glen blow his own nose without telling him which hand to use."

"He lets his son drive drunk, though, huh?" said Julie.

"Driving drunk," I said, "is evidently the way Glen asserts his independence."

Glen Falconer arrived about a quarter of seven and, as expected, Roger was with him. Julie escorted them both into my office and offered coffee, which we all accepted.

Roger and Glen sat beside each other on the sofa. I took the armchair across from them. "Paul Cizek will be here shortly," I said. "He's the miracle worker I mentioned."

"Cizek?" said Roger.

I nodded. "He's with Tarlin and Overton in Cambridge. He sort of specializes in *Mission Impossible* criminal cases. Which is what this one looks like."

Roger leaned forward. "What kind of name is Cizek?"

"Huh?"

"I said—"

"I heard what you said, Roger," I said. "I just didn't believe it."

"We don't want some sleazy—"

"Gotcha," I said quickly. I stood up, went to my desk, and buzzed Julie.

"I'm brewing some fresh coffee," she said over the intercom. "It'll be a few minutes."

"See if you can reach Paul Cizek," I said to her. "Tell him to forget it."

"Wait," said Glen.

"Hang on," I said to Julie. I looked at Glen. "Your father doesn't want a lawyer with a *Z* and a *K* in his last name defending you."

"You don't understand," said Roger.

"Of course I understand," I said. "I understand perfectly. It's really not that complicated."

"I didn't say—"

"You said enough."

Glen glanced at his father, then said, "I don't care what the man's name is. I need somebody good. I don't care if he's sleazy, as long as he's good."

"What's it going to be, gentlemen?" I said.

"Why don't you tell us about him," said Roger.

"Here's what you need to know," I said. "You asked me to get Glen a lawyer. I have done that. Paul Cizek happens to be a good friend of mine. I'm his family lawyer, just like I'm yours, although that's not relevant here. More to the point, Paul's simply the best lawyer in Boston for Glen's case, in my professional opinion. You have retained me because you are willing to pay me money to hear my professional opinion on the legal matters that present themselves to you. My opinion on legal matters is arguably more acute than yours, or else you would not have retained me. Ergo, your choices

18

are to accept or to reject my opinion. Which is your choice, S
ator?"

Roger stared at me for a moment, then smiled. "You never c
me 'Senator,' " he said.

"Only when you piss me off, and even then rarely to your face.'

"I guess I do piss people off sometimes. Sometimes I do it on pur–
pose. Sometimes it just happens. I like it best when people tell me
up front that they're pissed at me. That's why I like you." He
sighed. "I'm sorry, Brady. I value your opinion. It's more reliable
than mine. Your opinion is worth money to me."

"So?"

"So maybe we need a lawyer with unusual consonants in his last
name."

"Julie?" I said to the intercom.

"I'm listening," she said.

"Cancel the call to Paul."

"Aye, aye, Captain."

I went back and sat across from Glen and Roger. "I would've
kicked you both right the hell out of here if you'd started that dis-
cussion in front of Paul," I said to Roger.

"Times keep changing, Brady," he said. "I'm an old man. I have
trouble keeping up."

"You have trouble keeping your prejudices to yourself, and
you've got to try harder." I turned to Glen. "Paul Cizek is a helluva good lawyer, and he's on a roll lately. About a year ago he defended a guy accused of molesting the children at a day-care place
in Arlington—"

"Jesus," said Glen. "I remember that one. It was all over the news.
Guy name of Benson."

"Actually it was Benton," I said. "Victor Benton."

"Right," said Glen. "Benton."

"Never heard of him," said Roger.

"He made films," Glen said. "Kiddie porn. Little kids, they were,
grammar school. He made them undress at rest time, told them to—
to do things to each other. Sometimes he did things with them. He
got it on his camcorder, made tapes, sold them in Canada. That's

what he was accused of, anyway. They thought they had the guy absolutely nailed." Glen turned to me. "This Cizek, he's the one who got Benton off?"

"Paul negotiated a plea bargain," I said. "Now the guy's doing community service and seeing a shrink. As long as he stays out of the day-care business and away from little kids, he's a free man."

"He would've lasted about a week in prison," said Glen.

"Not many lawyers could've gotten Victor Benton off," I said. I looked directly at Roger. "Paul has done some work for the Russo family, too."

Roger's eyebrows went up. "Russo," he said. "They're—"

"Mafia," said Glen. "I remember a recent case. A hit man, wasn't it? It was all over the television. Was that Cizek, too?"

"That was Paul Cizek," I said.

"He got the man off," said Glen. "The DA thought he had an airtight case. But they ended up with a hung jury."

"Paul Cizek is very good at what he does," I said.

"I want this guy," said Glen.

Roger had been sitting there frowning. "Child molesters and Mafia hit men?" he said softly. "This is the man to defend a Falconer?"

"No, Roger," I said. "This is the man to defend a drunk driver by any name. Listen. He's not defending you, and he's not defending your family name. He's defending Glen, who got loaded, not for the first time, and climbed into his car and drove it into another car and killed a woman. Paul might not be able to win the case. But if anybody can, it's Paul Cizek. That's my opinion. Okay?"

"Sure, Brady." He shrugged. "Okay."

Julie brought in a tray with a carafe of coffee, three mugs, sugar, and milk. She placed it on the low table beside me and said, "Anything else?"

"That's great," I said. "When Paul gets here, just bring him in."

Julie turned and left the room. Glen followed her with his eyes.

I filled the three mugs with coffee, sipped from mine, and lit a cigarette. "Just so you don't embarrass me in front of Paul with more

irrelevancies," I said to Roger, "there are some other things you probably should know. Paul did not go to Harvard or Yale or Princeton. Not BC or BU, even. His old man was an immigrant Polish cobbler in Medford who was disabled by a stroke when Paul was fifteen and didn't die for another five years. His mother was a checkout clerk at K Mart and cleaned office buildings at night to put food on the table for Paul and his four siblings. Paul commuted to UMass Boston, then got his law degree from Suffolk, part-time. It took him about ten years to get through college and law school. He earned his way by waiting tables and tending bar at Italian restaurants in the North End, and probably met a lot of future clients in the process. The Middlesex County DA hired him for about fifteen grand a year to handle a caseload that would overwhelm an entire State Street firm. Within two years Paul Cizek was prosecuting homicides and getting convictions at an astounding rate. All the fancy downtown firms courted him, but he went to Tarlin and Overton in Cambridge because they wanted to keep him in front of juries, where he belonged. He's been with them almost five years. Paul's about forty now. He's got a nice house in Lynnfield and a Boston Whaler and a wife who went to Wellesley, who's a lawyer herself." I paused. "Let's see. Anything else I should tell you before he gets here?"

"He sounds like our man," said Roger.

"I hope you won't be startled by his appearance," I said.

He shook his head and shrugged.

I smiled. "But you probably will be."

I figured Roger had Paul Cizek pegged as a fat, big-nosed, toothpick-chewing caricature of a sleazy defense lawyer, a swarthy, foreign-looking man in a shiny suit with red suspenders and a flowery necktie and pointy shoes. In fact, Paul had fair skin, blond hair, ice-blue eyes, and the chiseled features of Butch Cassidy—or maybe it was the Sundance Kid. The Newman character.

When Julie escorted Paul into my office, Roger, to his credit, didn't blink. Paul was wearing chino pants and a cableknit sweater under an expensive tweed jacket. He shook hands graciously all around, declined Julie's offer of coffee, then said, "I'll need to talk to Glen for a few minutes."

I touched Roger's arm. "He means alone," I said.

Roger looked up. "Huh? Oh, sure."

Roger and I went out to my reception area, and about ten minutes later Paul and Glen came out.

"Okay," said Paul to me.

"You'll take the case?"

He shrugged. "I like challenges."

4

Thanksgiving, Christmas, New Year's Eve. Celebrations of family and tradition and peace and love and hope.

In the decade since Gloria and I had split, I had been finding the entire season disorienting and depressing and lonely, and I always greeted the arrival of the new year with relief because it marked the end of the holidays.

This year Alex made it different. At her insistence, we cooked a Thanksgiving turkey with stuffing and squash and sweet potatoes and giblet gravy and cranberry sauce and mince pie, and my old friends Charlie and Sarah McDevitt came over to share it with us. Then Alex bought a tree for my apartment, and we decorated it with homemade strings of popcorn and cranberries. On Christmas Eve we ate chili and drank eggnog and sang along to the entire *Messiah* and talked to my sons on the telephone and made love, and on New Year's Eve we drank champagne and watched the ball descend over Times Square on television, and the next day I realized that I'd made it through the whole time without once feeling disoriented or lonely or depressed.

It was a revelation.

★   ★   ★

I was staring out my office window at a cloudless January sky and dreaming of trout rivers and mayflies when Julie buzzed me. "Mr. Cizek, line two," she said.

I hit the button and said, "I was just counting the weeks until I might go fishing. I ran out of fingers."

"Try not to think about it," he said. "Better yet, let me buy you a beer."

"That might help. When?"

"Tonight? Say around six?"

"None too soon. Name the place."

"Skeeter's."

"I'll be there."

I had talked to Paul a couple of times after the November meeting in my office, when he agreed to take Glen Falconer's case. I'd filled him in on Glen's legal and personal history and given him a few tips on dealing with Roger, whom he had instantly pegged as an obtrusive pain in the ass. The week after Thanksgiving a Middlesex County grand jury handed down an indictment, as expected, and Glen Falconer's trial was scheduled to begin the first week of February.

When the indictment came in, the *Globe* ran Alex's story on the bottom left of page five, without a photo. She had been assigned to cover the trial and kept me updated on the case. Her boss had not at first seemed especially intrigued with the human-interest appeal of the Falconer story. Alex and I both suspected that the tentacles of Roger's influence had wiggled into the *Globe*'s editorial offices. But gradually the juicy details of the Falconer family history and the tragedy of the fatal automobile collision found their way into her stories.

Glen had been ignored and emotionally abused as a child, while his high-profile father bought and sold in the marketplace of influence and power and tyrannized his wife and son. No wonder Paul became an alcoholic ne'er-do-well as an adult.

Otherwise, the plight of the Falconer family had not occupied me. I had other things on my mind, trivial questions such as, What's it all about? and Who cares anyway?

Alex kept saying we should both quit our jobs, load all our stuff into a truck, and head for Montana. I kept wondering why I always tried to change the subject.

On one especially dismal winter day shortly after the arrival of the new year, I was having lunch at Marie's with Charlie McDevitt. I mentioned how I'd been finding myself preoccupied with how I might squeeze maximum enjoyment from my remaining years of mortality. "I feel like I'm coasting through life," I told Charlie. "I need a plan. Some days I just want to chuck it all and go live in a cabin out West with Alex."

"You want to give God a big chuckle?" said Charlie.

"Huh?"

"Just tell Him you've got plans," he said.

I left the office around five-thirty. The city was dark and bone-chilling cold. The wind off the water funneled between the buildings and knifed into my body. I walked briskly, hunched into my topcoat, up Boylston, past the Public Gardens, diagonally across the Common, left on Tremont, and then down Court Street to the alley off State Street to Skeeter's Infield.

I walked in, rubbed the cold out of my palms, and looked around. The bar was crowded and the early sports news was playing on the two big television sets at the ends. Skeeter was hustling behind the bar. When he saw me he lifted his chin in greeting.

Paul wasn't at the bar. I spotted him in the last booth. A short man in a camel-hair topcoat and felt hat was standing in the aisle, bent over with both hands on Paul's table. The man seemed to be talking intently. Paul was looking down into a glass of beer.

I went over to the booth. Paul glanced up, frowned for an instant, then said, "Oh, Brady. You're a little early."

I nodded. "Sorry. I walked fast. It's too damn cold out there to dawdle."

He smiled. "Don't be sorry. Have a seat."

The man who'd been talking to Paul straightened up, and I slipped into the booth across from Paul.

"Mr. Coyne," said Paul, tipping his head in the direction of the man in the camel-hair coat, "Mr. Vaccaro."

Mr. Vaccaro mumbled, "Hiya," without offering his hand, so I didn't offer mine.

"Mr. Vaccaro was just leaving," said Paul.

"Yeah," the man said to Paul. "We'll talk, though, huh, Mr. C.?"

"I'll think about what you've told me," said Paul. "Okay?"

"Sure. Sorry. I'm on my way. I just—we gotta talk sometime, you know what I mean?"

"I know what you mean, Eddie."

The man stood there for a moment, then shrugged, turned, and left.

Paul lifted his glass of dark beer and took a sip. "Nippy out there tonight," he said.

"Radiational cooling, they call it," I said. "Makes you wonder if this is the year spring will never come. Was that a client?"

"*Former* client." Paul looked toward the bar and lifted his hand, and a minute later Skeeter came over and placed a bottle of Sam Adams in front of me. "Howya doin' tonight, Mr. Coyne?" he said.

"Cold of limb and cold of heart," I said.

"Ain't it the way, though." He pointed at Paul's glass. "You okay, Mr. Cizek?"

Paul gave him a wave. "Fine for now, Skeets."

After Skeeter went back to his post behind the bar, I lit a cigarette and said, "So what's up, Paul? It's been a while."

"If my fucked-up sense of ethics didn't forbid it," he said, "I'd dump this damn Falconer case."

"Roger bothering you?"

He ran his fingers through his hair. "Not anymore. I fired the old bastard a month ago."

"You fired him?"

"Yep. He raised the bail, and that was fine, but I guess he figured that entitled him to plan the defense."

"I suspect he's not pleased with the kind of ink he's been getting," I said mildly.

"I'm just trying to win a case," said Paul. "If he cares more for his own image than whether his son spends the next ten years at MCI Concord, we should just plead guilty and take what they give us. I don't even ask my clients for their advice on how to run a trial, never mind their relatives. I guess Roger's not used to not being consulted. He second-guessed every move I made, and as polite as I tried to be to him, I finally just had it up to here. Told him I didn't want to see him ever again. Told him the next time he showed up with Glen, I was outta there. Surprised he didn't go running to you. I think you're the only person he listens to."

I shrugged. "He knows what I would've told him."

Paul sipped his beer. "I don't like Glen, either. He's got this attitude like it's a big nuisance, him being put on trial, and who the hell did that woman think she was, out there with her baby getting in the way, while he was exercising his God-given right as an American citizen to get shitfaced and barrel around in his car. I mean, yeah, I've gotta try to shift the blame. That's basic strategy. But I'd feel a lot better if the guy showed a little remorse. Bottom line, he killed a woman."

"Sorry I got you involved," I said. "I just figured you were the best man for the job."

He waved his hand dismissively. "I probably am," he said. "Anyway, it's not the old Senator, and it's not Glen, and it's not really even this case, and I don't know why I'm crying on your shoulder." He let out a deep breath and looked up at me. "Except I guess I don't feel like crying on Olivia's shoulder anymore."

"Uh-oh."

"Nah, it's not what you're thinking. She's okay. It's just me. Listen. I remember you telling me that once upon a time you wanted to be a civil liberties lawyer."

I smiled. "That was a long time ago. Law school and youthful idealism. A deadly combination."

He nodded. "Sure. And now you've got a practice that's the envy of every lawyer in the city."

"I haven't had a civil liberties case in my entire career, Paul. It's always been a regret. And somehow I doubt that you envy my practice."

"In lots of ways I do," he said. "I mean, you've got to coddle people like Roger Falconer, and that's no fun. But look at what I do."

"You perform miracles, Paul. That Benton case—"

"Yeah, exactly. I performed a miracle, and now that goddamn sodomist is walking the streets."

"Sodomist? With children? Jesus." I shook my head. "I knew about the pornographic videotapes. But I never heard anything about sodomy."

"It never came out in the trial." Paul nodded. "I managed to get the whole sodomy thing suppressed. You know. Tainted evidence, shoddy investigation, impeachable witnesses. Typical." He shrugged. "See what I mean? That's what I do. I put child sodomists back on the streets."

I sipped my beer and gazed at him. "I get it," I said. "You're afraid you're going to win this case and Glen Falconer will be free to get drunk and smash his car into somebody else."

"Sure. Absolutely. And he will, too. But that ain't exactly it, either." He leaned across the table. "I loved prosecuting, Brady. Prosecuting was straightforward and unambiguous, you know? Every single son of a bitch I went after had done something bad. My job was to prove it, to make the case, to convince the jury. When I succeeded, I knew I had made justice happen."

"And you practically always succeeded," I said. "Listen, old buddy. You're doing justice now, too, and you know it."

"Sure," he growled. "The right to counsel, the presumption of innocence, all that shit. But you know and I know that just because the law presumes somebody's innocent doesn't make him innocent. It's all just a fucking game, Brady. You go to trial to win the game, not to do justice. You play the media, you pick your best jury, you work on the judge. You wait for the prosecution to fuck up, or, even better, you sucker 'em into fucking up, and then you cram it down their throats. That's how it goes. If they don't fuck up, I lose. But they practically always fuck up somewhere along the line. Listen, how d'you think I felt when that foreman looked at Eddie Vaccaro standing there beside me and said, 'The jury cannot agree on a verdict,' huh?"

"Vaccaro," I said. "The guy who was just here?"

"Yeah, him."

"Jesus," I said. "I didn't make the connection. He's a hit man. I don't think I ever met a hit man before."

"You're not missing anything, Brady." Paul lifted his beer glass halfway to his mouth, then put it down. "Eddie Vaccaro shoots people for a living. The first bullet through the eyeball, then one behind the ear. That's his signature. By all rights, he should be doing life in Cedar Junction now. Instead the DA has pretty much given up going for a retrial. So Eddie Vaccaro's a free man. Back doing what he does best, I presume. Shooting people in the eye. Thanks to me."

"The thrill of victory," I said.

"Bullshit. I felt like I'd murdered that guy in the restaurant myself, just like bargaining Victor Benton down to community service made me feel like it was me who'd been sodomizing little kids. All the time I'm interrogating witnesses on the stand and challenging evidence and manipulating procedure, I'm thinking, Man, I wish I was prosecuting these miserable pricks instead of defending them. I wish I was putting them away rather than getting them off."

"Somebody—"

"Oh, yeah," he said quickly. "Somebody's got to do it. It's their right to counsel. Sure. You know, there are times I wish I wasn't so damn good at it. There are times it almost makes me cry to see an inept, inexperienced, overworked prosecutor up there trying to get my client convicted. I'm practically screaming to myself, 'No, you dumb schmuck. Don't put that witness up there. I'm gonna have to destroy that witness.' You know what I mean?"

I nodded.

He took a sip of beer. "God help me, Brady, sometimes I find myself rooting for the other side. There are times I almost wish I'd lose."

"Maybe you should go back to prosecuting."

"Yup, I think of that. Olivia and I could sell the house and sell the boat and sell her new Saab and sell most of our furniture and go back to the little apartment on Memorial Drive. Maybe after ten or fifteen years I could run for DA and stick my thumb into the political pie and make television statements and never have to go into a courtroom again until I lost an election."

I smiled and nodded. "Alex and I are talking about moving out West."

"Really?"

I shrugged. "I doubt it'll ever happen. But thinking about it sometimes makes it seem real, and that makes me feel better for a little while. It's an option. It makes me feel that there's a way out if it ever gets intolerable."

Paul looked up. Skeeter was standing by our booth. " 'Scuse me, men," he said, "but I wondered if you wanted a burger tonight? Or a refill?"

I glanced at Paul, and he nodded. "Burgers, Skeets," I said. "You know how we like 'em. And I'm ready for coffee."

"Coffee for me, too," said Paul.

Skeeter grinned and ambled away.

"I don't feel that way," said Paul after a minute. "I don't feel like I've got any options. Tarlin and Overton pays me a shitload of money, which they should considering how much I make for them. I like my house and I like my boat and I like my wife. I just . . . "

He shook his head, and I said, "You just what?"

He smiled quickly. "I guess I just don't like myself very much. Brady, God help me, I want to lose this case. I want Glen Falconer to spend ten years in prison. I want six big guys with tattoos all over their fat hairy bellies to ream his butt in the showers. And I want that sanctimonious old shit to spend the rest of his miserable life regretting the way he raised his son, and I want your Alex to drag the Falconer name through all the puke and slime she can find. That's what I want."

"If you feel that way, you should quit the case."

"The thing is," he said, "I can win. I expect to win. And I don't have it in me not to do my best to win."

"So that makes you the best lawyer for the case."

He nodded. "That's the problem."

"Just as I promised Glen."

"Sure. And all my vows and training forbid me from quitting just because I don't like the Falconers and don't like defending them. Nope. I've gotta see it through."

"I guess I don't know what to say, Paul."

"I didn't expect you to say anything, old buddy. I just expected you to listen and pretend to understand. Which you did."

"I didn't pretend," I said.

Skeeter brought our burgers, big, thick, juicy hunks of ground sirloin and half-melted slabs of cheddar between slices of toasted garlic bread. Between mouthfuls Paul told me he and Olivia were hoping to get away for two weeks after the Falconer trial. Someplace warm and distant from fax machines and cellular telephones, where there might be fish to catch and piña coladas to sip by the pool and where, they thought, they might try to make a baby.

"It's always fun to try, anyhow," he said, and by the time we had wiped all the burger juice off our chins and finished our coffee, Paul was waving his arms and drawing diagrams on the placemat and explaining to me how he expected the state to focus on Glen's Breathalyzer results, and how he knew he could raise enough reasonable doubt to deep-six the prosecution's entire case.

We huddled in our topcoats outside Skeeter's. "I'm parked in the garage," Paul said. "Want a lift?"

"I'll walk," I said. "Penance for Skeeter's burger."

He held out his hand and I took it. "Thanks," he said.

"What for? You paid."

"I feel better. You got me back on track."

"I didn't say anything, Paul."

He grinned. "Just talking with somebody who's as fucked up as me helps."

"I guess you came to the right man, then."

5

When I was a kid, we celebrated our national holidays—Columbus Day, Armistice Day, George Washington's Birthday—on the days when they actually occurred. As soon as the new calendars were printed I thumbed through them to see if I was going to get gypped out of a no-school day because one of the holidays fell on a Saturday that year. I didn't like it when it happened that way. But it never occurred to me to think of it as unfair. Holidays came when they did and, like most things, you took 'em when you got 'em.

Somewhere along the line they decided to homogenize and regularize our holidays. No longer do we celebrate the signing of the armistice that ended the Great War on November 11 (the eleventh hour of the eleventh day of the eleventh month, I recall my third-grade teacher, Mrs. Shattuck, telling us). Now we're supposed to call it "Veteran's Day." And now kids are excused from school on Mondays, regardless of when October 12 or February 22 happen to fall. Instead of commemorating Washington's birthday, we celebrate something called "Presidents' Day," honoring not only the father of our country but also Franklin Pierce and Warren G. Harding and Gerald Ford.

I've questioned a lot of school-age kids, and I have yet to find one who can tell me the historical significance of November 11. A lot of them are even cynical about the fact that George Washington never told a lie. I asked my son Billy about it once, back when he was in junior high, and he said, "Oh, nobody believes that cherry tree story. It's a myth. Everybody tells lies, Pop."

I don't know what they're teaching kids nowadays.

The word *verdict* derives from the Latin roots meaning "to tell the truth." So it was appropriate that on the morning of February 22, the birthday of the man who, I still like to think, always told the truth (but a Thursday this year and therefore not Presidents' Day), Alex called me from a pay phone at the Middlesex County Courthouse, where she had been following the Falconer trial. "They expect the jury to bring back their verdict this afternoon," she said. "Why don't you meet me for lunch and then join me in the courtroom for the show?"

"Lunch sounds good," I said, "but why should I want to watch them announce the verdict? It's not as if I haven't been inside courtrooms."

"I just figured, Glen Falconer's really your client, and Paul Cizek is your friend. The Senator's been in the front row the whole time, you know, mostly glaring at Cizek and trying to make eye contact with Glen. I suspect he'd appreciate your show of support."

"What's the buzz?" I asked.

"Hard to judge. Cizek destroyed the Breathalyzer witness, and he made some points with the crime scene evidence. He scored on the fact that the victim was not wearing a seat belt, too, and raised some very reasonable doubt, some are saying, about whether the woman was driving safely herself. He's created some sympathy for Glen, too, mostly at the expense of Roger. Abusive father and husband creates mentally disordered wife and neurotic, alcoholic son. I don't think anybody doubts Falconer was drunk and ran into her, though. It'll be interesting. Cizek's been a tiger, and there's no doubt that the jurors love him."

"What do you think?" I asked her.

"I think he's absolutely adorable."

"I meant," I said, "how do you think it'll turn out? The verdict?"

"I'm just a reporter, honey. I'm not supposed to speculate."

During the course of the trial, which had lasted into a third week, Alex had kept me updated. I had tried to root for Paul to win and for Glen Falconer, who was, after all, the son of one of my important clients, to be exonerated. But something in me kept hoping that Glen would get nailed. I hate drunk drivers, and I hate seeing people elude justice because they happen to have more money and influence than other folks.

"It'll probably be a circus, huh?" I said to Alex.

"Probably. Everybody loves a circus."

"Pretty girls in spangled leotards?"

"Oh, yes. The place is packed with them. I've got mine on."

"Okay. Lunch it is. I'll have Julie clear my afternoon. The usual place?"

"I'll see you there at noon."

There's a little bar and grill around the corner from the courthouse in east Cambridge where we lawyers and reporters and other regulars go for lunch. It was mobbed. Alex and I ate BLTs and drank coffee at the bar and could barely converse over the din. Everybody seemed to be arguing about the Falconer case. I inferred that many drinks and a lot of dollars were being wagered on the verdict.

Shortly after Alex and I squeezed onto benches near the front of the courtroom, Paul and Glen came in and sat at the defendant's table. I saw Roger's bald head in the first row directly behind them.

Alex pointed toward the prosecution table. "See that man?" she said. "The guy with the beard in the front row?"

I followed her finger. "Who's he?"

"The husband of the victim. He's been giving interviews to anybody who'll listen to him. You've probably seen him on the news."

"You know I hardly ever watch the news."

She squeezed my hand. "Right. And you don't read newspapers much, either."

"Just your stuff."

"Of course. For its literary qualities. Anyway, keep an eye on him. His name is Thomas Gall, and if you ask him, he'll tell you that the credibility of the entire American system of justice rests on the outcome of this case."

"Meaning what?"

She shrugged. "He just says that the jury had better find Falconer guilty."

"Sounds like a threat."

"Actually," said Alex, "it sounds like a man who is devastated over the random loss of his wife to a drunk driver."

"I can relate to that," I said.

"Sure," she said. "Everybody can."

A little after two o'clock the jury filed in. Paul and Glen stood and faced them.

"Have you reached a verdict?" said the judge.

The foreman, actually a forewoman with gray hair wearing a severe black dress, stood and said, "We have, Your Honor."

A moment later the words "not guilty" were drowned in a cacophony of groans, cheers, shouts, and cries. Down front I saw Glen grab Paul's arm and pump his hand. Roger had both arms raised in a victory salute. Reporters were crowding the aisles and pushing toward the doors. The repeated banging of the judge's gavel had no perceptible effect on the chaos.

I felt Alex's fingernails dig into my wrist. "Look," she said.

She was pointing at Thomas Gall. He was a thick-necked, black-bearded man wearing a corduroy sport jacket over a blue oxford shirt without a necktie, and he was shouldering through the crowd in the direction of the defense table. His teeth were bared and his eyes were narrowed and he was shaking his right fist in the air. I saw his mouth moving, and then his words rose above the general din of the courtroom.

"This ain't done with, you murderin' son of a bitch," he yelled, raising his arm above the crowd and jabbing his forefinger toward Glen. "You neither, you creep." This was directed at Paul Cizek. And then Gall turned dramatically, lifted his arm, and pointed at the judge. "Or you," he growled, and, taking in the jury with a sweep of his hand, "or you, neither, all of you."

Alex mumbled, "Meet me outside," and slipped into the aisle. I saw her working her way toward Gall, but a pair of uniformed police officers got to him first. They pinned his arms by his sides and half-carried him out a side door.

I waited in my seat, and after a while the hubbub died down. I stood up and went to the front of the courtroom. I didn't spot Alex, but Glen and Paul were seated at the defense table. Paul was leaning forward, talking intently, and Glen was sitting back, his arms folded across his chest. He was staring up at the ceiling, nodding now and then. Roger was standing with both hands gripping the barrier rail, watching them.

Brenda, Glen's wife, sat on the front-row bench a few spaces away from Roger. Her blond hair was twisted into some kind of a fancy bun on the back of her head, and she wore a pale blue business suit over a silky white blouse with a frilly collar. She held her hands folded quietly in her lap, and she seemed to be studying the decor of the courtroom. I leaned down to her and said, "Congratulations."

She looked up, frowned for just an instant of nonrecognition, then smiled quickly. "Oh, hello."

"Brady Coyne," I said. "We—"

"Yes, I remember."

"You must be pleased with the verdict," I said stupidly.

"Sure." She shrugged. "I guess so."

I frowned, and she cocked her head and met my eyes levelly for a moment. Hers, I noticed, were greenish blue, the same color as her suit.

"It must've been hard for you," I said. "Sitting through all this."
"Hard?"

I shrugged. "Not knowing how it would turn out."

"Mr. Coyne," she said with a smile, "everything always turns out right for the Falconer men." She held my eyes for a moment and then returned her gaze to the front wall of the courtroom.

I stood there for a moment, but it was clear that my conversation with Brenda had ended. I turned to Roger and touched his arm. "So what do you think?" I said.

He turned. "Oh, Brady. What brings you here?"

"Loyalty."

He smiled thinly. "Right. Good of you."

"I understand Paul Cizek has performed some miracles these past couple of weeks."

"Your Paul Cizek is a crude, disrespectful man who allowed the newspapers to turn this into a circus. He refused to communicate with me and I should have fired him."

"Except you weren't his client."

He shook his head. "No. Glen was his client. But I'm paying. When I'm paying, I expect to participate."

I shrugged. "Just as well you didn't fire him. He got the job done, I'd say."

"Yes, he did. By dragging in the family's private affairs, resurrecting the memory of Glen's absent mother and his father's deficient parenting and his entire neglectful upbringing. He had that jury feeling sorrier for my poor, misguided son than they did for the dead woman."

"I heard he was pretty good with the prosecution witnesses, too," I said.

Roger nodded. "Yes, there was that. We won, and I'm glad. And after the party, we'll never have to deal with Mr. Cizek again, and I'm glad about that as well."

"Planning a big celebration, are you?"

He turned to me, and once again Roger Falconer's famous senatorial smile spread across his face. "A small celebration, Brady. And you must come."

I shrugged. "Well . . . "

"I insist. You deserve much of the credit for our, um, victory."

I nodded. There was no tactful way I could get out of it. "Sure. I'll be there."

"And bring your little friend with you."

"My little friend?"

"Miss Shaw, the reporter. She *is* your friend, isn't she?"

"Yes, I suppose that's one of the things she is to me."

"Just tell her no interviews in my home."

"Oh, Alex is a cultured and respectful person, Senator. She knows how to behave."

He touched my shoulder. "I'm sorry, Brady. I forget my manners sometimes. It's been a difficult time."

"Well, it's over, and if you haven't thanked Paul Cizek you are certainly forgetting your manners."

He gave me his smile again. "Of course. He did a magnificent job." He reached for my hand and shook it. "Tomorrow evening, eight o'clock."

"I wouldn't miss it," I lied.

6

Floodlights glittered on the newest layer of February snow, and more was filtering down softly. The gunmetal gray Range Rover and the little white Mercedes two-seater were pulled up directly by the front porch of the Falconer house in Lincoln, precisely where they'd been the last time I'd been there.

A dozen or fifteen vehicles were parked in an area that had been cleared by a snowplow next to the circular driveway. I pulled into an empty space and turned off the engine.

Alex touched the back of my neck. "Let's have a cigarette before we go in."

"Are we nervous?"

"We are not nervous," she said. "We are simply not looking forward to this."

"None of us is. We shall pay our respects, or whatever you call it, and we shall depart as quickly as possible."

We lit cigarettes. Alex is one of those oddly nonaddictive people who can smoke a cigarette now and then and enjoy it enormously, without ever getting hooked. She laid her cheek on my shoulder. The windows inside my car began to fog over. "We could just stay here and make out," she murmured.

"Your clothing will become all disheveled, and your lipstick will get smeared, and what will your mother say?"

"Valid point. We mustn't make out. Maybe just grope a little."

We smoked in silence for a few minutes. "What's bothering you?" I said.

"I just hate these things."

"This has nothing to do with the editorial in today's *Globe,* then."

"The one criticizing the prosecution of the Falconer case? The one calling for a new look at the Commonwealth's record in convicting drunk drivers? The one that practically declared Glen Falconer a public enemy?"

"That's the one I had in mind," I said.

"Why should that make me wish I were home with you wearing sweats and playing Trivial Pursuit and drinking beer on a snowy Friday in February rather than all high-heeled and panty-hosed at a party full of people I don't know and don't even want to know?"

"Because it was you who wrote the editorial?"

"That was the paper's editorial, Brady. It was unsigned, because it was the opinion of the editorial staff."

"But you wrote it."

I heard her chuckle beside me in the darkness of the front seat of the car. "So what'd you think of it?"

"Awfully convincing, hon. Don't worry about it. Nobody in there will know you wrote it."

"Somehow I think Roger Falconer knows everything."

"Well, he's too cultured to say anything. Besides, even Roger Falconer can see the truth in what you said."

Alex stubbed her cigarette out in the ashtray, and I followed suit.

"Gimme a kiss," she said.

I did. It lasted a good long time.

Finally she turned on the dome light and squinted into the rearview mirror. She touched up her lipstick, then said, "Lemme see your face."

I turned to her and she dabbed at my mouth with a tissue. Then she planted a very gentle kiss on the tip of my nose.

"Okay," she said. "Let's get this over with."

Roger greeted us at the door. I was relieved to see that he was wearing a Harris tweed jacket over a dark green turtleneck. Black tie wouldn't have surprised me, and I was still in my office pinstripe.

He gripped my hand. "Brady, damn good of you to come," he said. I guessed he had been using the identical greeting for everybody who had arrived at his door that evening. Nevertheless, Roger made it sound personal and sincere. Sounding personal and sincere regardless of how he actually felt was one of the many talents that had made Roger Falconer a big-time politician and successful businessman.

"Good of you to invite us," I replied. I doubted if I sounded as sincere as Roger. I turned to Alex. "Alex, this is Roger Falconer. Roger, you know Alexandria Shaw?"

He took her extended hand in both of his. "Ah, yes. I've enjoyed your work, Miss Shaw. You're a fine writer. Your coverage of my son's trial has been most, um, objective."

Alex dipped her head and smiled. "Thank you, Mr. Falconer."

Roger took our coats and led us into the living room. A bar had been set up along one wall, and on the opposite side of the room was a long table holding hors d'oeuvres. A couple dozen people stood in clumps. "Help yourself to drinks," said Roger. "Brady, may I borrow Miss Shaw for a moment? There's somebody I'd like her to meet."

Alex rolled her eyes at me, gave her head a tiny shake, and mouthed the word "please."

"Sure, Roger," I said, ignoring her.

As Roger steered her away, she turned and stuck out her tongue at me.

I made my way to the bar. A college-aged girl wearing a white shirt and a black skirt stood behind it. "Like a drink, sir?"

"A Coke, please. I'm the designated driver."

She cocked her head at me, then grinned. She poured some Coke over a glass of ice cubes, and as she leaned across the table to hand it to me, she whispered, "I think it's disgusting, don't you?"

I gazed around the room. Just about everybody was holding a wine or highball glass or a beer bottle. After consuming free booze at the party celebrating Glen Falconer's exoneration from a vehicular homicide DUI charge, they would all climb into their cars and drive over the twisting, snow-slicked back roads of Lincoln.

"I don't know about disgusting," I said to the girl. "But it's pretty damn ironic."

"I lost two friends in high school," she said.

I nodded. "I used to lie awake every night when one of my sons was out in a car. Now they're away from home, and I only lie awake sometimes."

She hugged herself. "It's good money."

"I don't blame you," I said.

I felt a tug on my sleeve. I turned and found myself mashed in a strong embrace. A big wet kiss landed directly on my mouth.

"Oh," I said when she pulled back from me to give me a look at her. "Mary. What're you doing here?"

"I heard you'd be here, you sexy man." She grabbed my arm in both of hers. "Frankly," she whispered, "I am delighted to see a familiar face. Doc said we had to come, and I told him he could go right ahead, but he insisted I come too, and now he's off pontificating about impactions or occlusions or something. Probably to a bevy of beautiful young women. Gee, it's good to see you."

"How do you guys know the Falconers?"

"Oh, you know," she said. "Dr. Charles Adams, the oral surgeon for the wealthy and influential. Kinda like you're the lawyer for all of them."

"A lot of Doc's patients are my clients, it's true. So how's he doing? I haven't seen him for a while."

"Oh, he's full of wanderlust as usual. He wants to buy another motorcycle. I keep waiting for him to grow up."

"Don't hold your breath," I said.

I felt a hand on my elbow. "Excuse me, Brady."

I turned. Paul Cizek stood beside me.

I grabbed his hand and shook it. "Hey, congratulations," I said.

He nodded. "Sure. Thanks." To Mary he said, "Will you excuse me? I need to talk to Brady."

She shrugged. "That's okay."

"Have you two met?" I said.

Mary smiled at Paul. "I've seen you on television. I'm Mary Adams."

They shook hands. Then Paul and I excused ourselves. He gripped my arm and guided me into Roger's library. Nobody was there except the goldens, Abe and Ike, who were snoring and snuffling, each on his own leather sofa. The lights were low and a fire crackled in the fireplace. We sat in the same armchairs that Roger and Glen had been sitting in when I had been summoned to Lincoln back in November.

"What's up?" I said.

"I gotta talk to somebody."

"You want a lawyer or a shrink?"

"I don't know. Both, maybe."

"There's a top-notch oral surgeon here," I said. Then I looked at him. His knee was jiggling and frown lines creased his forehead. I touched his arm. "I'm sorry, Paul," I said. "You *are* upset. What is it?"

"I don't know. I got this big empty sucking feeling in my belly. It's been there for awhile. It keeps getting bigger and emptier."

"You feel bad about the Falconer trial, huh?"

"That, yeah. It was like winning a ten-to-nothing baseball game, you know? You wish they'd get a few runs, make it close, at least. The prosecution did a lousy job, Brady. Hell, it was a game I should've lost, and the terrible thing is, I wish I did." He flapped his hands. "And then . . . "

His voice trailed away and he stared into the fireplace.

"Then what?" I said.

He turned to me and shrugged. "Olivia and I are a little shaky. More and more she's throwing all her frustration and energy into her work, and I guess I am, too." He hunched his shoulders and squeezed his hands between his knees. "It's all falling apart. I don't know what to do."

"Didn't you tell me you and Olivia were going to get away for a couple weeks after the trial? Head for some tropical place and relax? Make a baby, I thought you said."

"Yeah, well, we like to play with that fantasy sometimes. But she's decided she's got too much going on and can't leave right now."

"You don't need a lawyer, pal," I said.

"You think I do need a shrink, huh?"

"I don't know. Maybe you just need a little down time. Big cases take a lot out of you, and there's always that letdown when they're over. The agony of victory and all."

He looked up at me and smiled. "Postpartum blues."

"I wouldn't know about that."

"You were there yesterday, weren't you?" he said.

"I heard the jury give their verdict, sure. I wanted to shake your hand, but you disappeared with Glen."

"I had to get him out of there. That guy—"

"Gall? The husband of the victim? I heard him."

"He freaked Glen out of his wits."

"What about you?"

"Me?" Paul nodded. "Yeah, he kinda freaked me out, too. I mean, he didn't really scare me, but the poor bastard had to sit there and watch the case against the guy who killed his wife go swirling down the drain. Honestly, I felt bad for him. I can't blame him for being totally pissed. The hell of it is, it feels like it's my fault."

"People think a trial is supposed to reveal the truth," I said.

"It's just a lawyer contest," he said, "and I'm getting sick of it."

I sighed. "I don't know what to tell you, Paul."

"There's nothing to say. Thanks for listening."

"Let me get some names for you."

"Names?"

"Somebody to talk to."

He stared at me for a minute, then said, "Yeah. Okay." He stood up. "I've gotta get out of here."

"Did you bring Olivia?"

He shook his head. "She had some meeting or something." He shrugged. "We don't do much together anymore."

"I would've liked to see her."

"Some other time, I guess."

Paul and I walked out into the party. He turned and shook my hand. "We'll have to get together. Do some fishing."

"I'd like that," I said. "I'll be in touch with you."

Paul weaved his way through the crowd toward the front door. I looked around for Alex. Instead I saw Doc Adams coming toward me. "They let the hoi polloi into this affair, huh?" he said.

"Apparently," I said. "You're here."

He narrowed his eyes. "You got lipstick on your mouth."

"Your wife attacked me a little while ago. She seems sex starved."

"Must be, to go after an ugly son of a bitch like you. So what's new?"

"Actually," I said, "maybe you can help me. I could use a referral to a good psychiatrist."

"Midlife angst, counselor?"

"Well, yeah, sure. But it's not for me."

"Of course it isn't."

"Well, it's not. Can you get me a few names?"

"Can do," said Doc. "What about lunch? I'm at Mass General on Wednesdays and Thursdays."

"Sounds good. Give me a call." I scanned the room. "I'm ready to get out of here. Have you seen Alex around?"

He grinned. "Why, sure. I was holding her in thrall with a tale of a miraculous mandible reconstruction I performed last week. Young housewife whose husband smashed her face with his fist."

"Jesus," I said. "What a world."

"Amen," said Doc.

At that moment Alex appeared. "Hi," she said to me.

"Hi yourself."

"You got lipstick all over you. It's not mine."

"It was this guy's wife. She attacked me."

Alex put her arm around my waist. "I don't blame her."

Doc smiled at us. "Hard to believe," he said. "You give her a perfect opening and she doesn't insult you."

"Not in public," I said.

"And she's not jealous."

"Nope. She trusts me."

Doc grinned. "She'll get over it."

Alex squeezed my arm. "About ready to go, handsome?"

"Yes. Definitely. Have you seen Glen? I really ought to say hi to him."

"I haven't seen him," she said.

"I heard he refused to attend," said Doc. "I was talking to his wife."

I grinned. "You hit on all the women here?"

"Only the pretty ones. All she'd say was that Glen wasn't feeling well, which sounded to me like he was either in the bag or seriously hungover."

"In that case," I said to Alex, "we're out of here."

I had lunch with Doc Adams the following Thursday. He gave me a list of four psychiatrists. "They've got good reputations for helping men through depression and midlife anxieties," Doc said. "They're friends of mine. They're pretty booked, but they said they'd be willing to take on a new patient on my referral."

"Contrary to popular belief," I said, "you are a kind and thoughtful man."

"Jesus," he said. "Don't tell anybody. It'd ruin my reputation."

I called Paul Cizek's office that afternoon and left a message asking him to call me. A week passed and I called again. All his secretary would tell me was that he wasn't in his office. I repeated my message, adding that I had some names for him.

He didn't return that call, either. I tried him again a few weeks later, suggesting lunch, and again a month or so after that.

He never returned any of my phone calls. Winter turned into spring and the leaves began to pop out and the days lengthened and I stopped trying to reach Paul Cizek. I thought I understood. He didn't want my help and regretted exposing his fears and weaknesses to me. When he wanted to get together, he'd let me know.

7

When I got home from the office on the first Friday in June, the sliding glass doors that gave me my view of the harbor were wide open and a damp east wind was whipping the curtains around.

I found Alex slouched on her spine in one of the aluminum chairs on the balcony. She'd taken off her shoes, and she had her legs stretched out in front of her with her heels propped on the railing. Her skirt was bunched up around her hips so that the wind could blow on her bare legs. She held a bottle of Samuel Adams on her chest, and she was staring out at the thunderheads that were building on the horizon in the fading daylight.

I bent and kissed her forehead. It tasted damp and salty. "You're gonna get wet," I said. "It's raining."

"It's not raining yet," she said, still gazing out at the roiling sky. The dark clouds were tinged with orange. "The wind is picking up water from the top of the ocean and blowing it around. It's refreshing. It feels tingly on my skin."

"You don't want to change your clothes? That's an expensive silk skirt you're ruining."

She took a long swig from her beer bottle, placed it on the concrete floor beside her, and returned her gaze to the sky. "I'm cool. I'm extremely cool. I'm wicked cool."

I noticed that there was a six-pack of Sam Adams on the floor beside her left elbow. Two unopened bottles were left in the cardboard container. "How long've you been here?" I said.

"I don't know. Ten minutes. A few hours. I forget. I've been watching the clouds. They're pretty awesome, don't you think? It's like there's this big guy out there at the edge of the ocean, and he's blowing up all these big black balloons. I can feel his wet breath on my legs when he blows. It feels good. And those balloons are getting bigger and bigger and they're filling up the sky, and I'm waiting for the sky to get so crowded with those big black clouds that they'll all explode." She held up her hands, then spread them wide apart. "Boom!"

"Let me change my clothes," I said. "I'll sit with you and watch the big guy blow up the balloons."

"Let's get naked." She stood, unsnapped her skirt, balled it up, and threw it over the rail. It opened in the wind, flapped like a big drunken bird, and sailed away. Then she turned to me and stripped off my jacket.

"No, wait," I said. "That's an expensive suit." I grabbed it from her and threw it into the living room behind me.

She yanked my necktie off and tossed it over the balcony. "Now do me," she said, and I unbuttoned her blouse while she worked on the buttons of my shirt, and both shirt and blouse went out into the storm. She wanted to sacrifice my pants to the guy who blew up the black balloons, but I snatched them from her and threw them inside, and then we were standing there, Alex in her pink bra and matching panties and me in my boxers, holding each other while the wind blew cold and wet on our skin. She trembled in my arms, and when I teased her chin up with the knuckle of my forefinger, I saw that she was crying.

I kissed both of her eyes. "What's the matter, honey?" I said.

"I guess I had too many beers."

"Okay. That's okay. You're entitled. Why did you have too many beers?"

She ducked her head against my chest and mumbled something. I bent to her ear. "I couldn't hear you."

She tilted up her face and looked at me. "I got it."

"You got what?"

"The contract. Sally called today. My agent. They sent her a contract."

"Hey," I said. "Slow down. What agent? What contract are you talking about?"

She slumped back into the chair. "I was going to tell you. But I was afraid it would be bad luck to talk about it. To want it. And I didn't know if I wanted it or not, anyway." She shivered. "I still don't."

I put my arm around her. "A contract for what, hon?"

"A book." She shivered. "They're giving me money to write a book."

I stood up and held my hands out to her. "Come on. Let's go inside, make some coffee, get some clothes on. I want to hear all about it."

Fifteen minutes later we were sipping hot coffee at the table. We'd changed into sweats, and on the other side of the sliding glass doors, the sky was full of dark clouds and it had begun to rain.

"Now," I said. "Tell me about your book."

Alex smiled quickly. "Remember that series I did on abused wives?"

I nodded. "Sure. There was Pulitzer talk, as I recall."

"Well, they want me to do a book on it. A different book. The publisher liked my slant. It looks at the dynamics that produce these abusive relationships."

"You mean how women drive men to it?"

She looked sharply at me, and I quickly held up my hand. "Joke, kid."

She nodded. "I know when you're joking. You're not always funny. It's about how mothers raise their boys to beat their wives, and how fathers raise their daughters to seek out abusive men to marry, and how abusers and victims seem to seek out and marry each other, and . . . " She shrugged. "Anyway," she said, "I got the contract. Sally called today."

"And that's why you drank more beers than usual and threw away your clothes."

"Yup. I'm gonna be a real writer. I'm sorry, Brady."

"Sorry? Why? This is wonderful news."

"I'm sorry I didn't tell you about it before."

I reached across the table and put my hand over hers. "That doesn't matter. Congratulations. It's an appropriate occasion to drink a lot of beers and discard your clothing."

She was shaking her head. "What if I can't do it? What if I spend the money they give me and I can't write anything? What if the paper dumps me and won't take me back?" Tears welled up in her eyes. "What if . . . "

I squeezed her hand. "I'm proud of you. You're going to write a wonderful book. You're a hard worker and a terrific writer. Publishers don't invest money in people who can't do the job."

"They don't know me like I do," she said.

When we finished our coffee, I took her hand and led her to the shower. We stripped off clothes and stood under the steaming water. Alex cried and pressed against me, and I held her tight until she whispered, "I'm okay now." I lathered her up all over and twirled her slowly under the hot spray. "Now your turn," she said, and she washed me. We toweled each other dry and then she took my hand and led me to the bedroom.

We made love. We dozed.

Sometime in the evening I awakened. Alex had her arm thrown across my chest and she was breathing softly on my cheek. I slipped away from her, pulled on a pair of jeans and a T-shirt, went into the kitchen, and dumped two cans of Progresso minestrone into a saucepan.

While it heated I smoked a cigarette and stared out the sliding door at the storm that raged over the harbor. Raindrops as big as acorns splattered against the glass. Six stories down, frothy white combers rolled across the black water. Now and then lightning lit up the sky.

I felt Alex press herself against my back. "I love a big storm," she whispered.

"It reminds us who's boss."

"Yes. It puts things into perspective."

"I've got some soup heating on the stove."

She snaked her hand under my T-shirt and rubbed my chest. "So what if I can't do the dumb book," she said.

"You can do it."

"I think I can."

"We should be celebrating," I said.

"We already did."

"That was it?"

She chuckled. "No. That was just the prologue. Let's have some soup. Then we can celebrate some more."

Later we lay in the dark staring up at the ceiling. "I'm sorry for acting like a female hysteric," Alex murmured.

"I think that's a redundancy."

"What is?"

" 'Female hysteric.' The word *hysteria* comes from the Greek word for 'uterus.' Originally, at least, they thought only females were susceptible to hysteria."

"Because they had a uterus," said Alex.

"Because they were female, which was more or less defined as having a uterus."

"Males didn't have hysteria."

"No," I said. "Being deprived of uteruses and all. When males had those symptoms, they figured there was really something wrong with them."

"The doctors giving those diagnoses being predominantly male."

"Exclusively male back then, I believe," I said.

She rolled onto her side and kissed my shoulder. "I'll have to move," she said softly. "I'll need a quiet place. In the country, probably. Maine, maybe, or Vermont. Someplace cheaper. I'll have to get a leave from the paper, and I'll have to live on the advance for two years, and anyway, I *want* to move. But . . . "

"I understand," I said.

"Do you? It'll be someplace not—not so near to you."

"We'll work it out."

"I've been thinking," she said.

"What have you been thinking?"

"You could come with me. It wouldn't be Montana, but . . . "

"It's something to think about," I said quietly.

We lay there in silence for a few minutes. Then Alex said, "Brady?"

"What, hon?"

"You're more important to me than a book, you know?"

I didn't say anything.

"Hey?"

"Mmm?"

"Did I say something wrong?"

I hugged her against me. "Sometimes you think too much," I said.

"I want you to be happy."

"Me, too," I said. "I want both of us to be happy."

When both of my sons fled the East Coast for Western time zones, I stopped being frightened when the phone awakened me in the middle of the night. Billy liked to tell me about the trout he was catching in Idaho. Rubbing it in, I called it, but I was always happy to hear from him, even if it did interrupt my sleep. Joey called less often and less spontaneously than his brother, but as smart as he was, he always seemed surprised when I reminded him that eleven o'clock in the evening in California was 2:00 A.M. in Boston.

So when the telephone shrilled in the dark that night, it didn't jar me upright in bed the way it used to when the boys were still teenagers living with Gloria and my first waking thought was of automobile accidents.

I fumbled for the phone, got it after the second ring, and held it to my ear. "H'lo?"

"Brady?" It was neither of my sons. Billy calls me Pop and Joey

52

calls me Dad, and both of them generally call me collect. Anyway, this voice was female.

"Yes, this is Brady," I mumbled.

"It's Olivia."

"Oh . . . ?"

"Olivia Cizek. You were the first person I thought of to call. I'm sorry to wake you up."

"It's okay." I bunched my pillow behind me and pushed myself into a semi-sitting position. Beside me Alex twitched and groaned. "What's the matter?" I said softly into the phone.

"It's very strange. It's . . . "

"Olivia, are you okay?"

"I don't know. I—the Coast Guard just called. They found Paul's boat."

"What do you mean?"

I heard her exhale a loud breath. "His boat. It was drifting somewhere out around the Merrimack River. They towed it in, and then they called me, and—"

"Where's Paul?"

"I don't know." She hesitated, then said, "Oh. You probably don't know, do you?"

"Know what?"

I heard her take a breath. "Paul and I separated a couple months ago, Brady."

"I didn't know," I said. "I'm sorry."

"He's been living up there. On Plum Island. Since we—we split. Up there in that—he calls it a shack. They called here for him. They got the numbers off the boat and this was the address, but—"

"Olivia, listen," I said. "We've had a big storm tonight. Paul's boat broke away from its moorings, that's all. Call him and tell him what happened. He's pretty lucky they found it in this storm. It could've been sunk or gone halfway to Labrador."

"I tried calling him. There was no answer." She paused. "You don't get it," she said.

"What do you mean?"

"He doesn't keep his boat moored. He trailers it. Do you understand?"

Alex mumbled something and rolled toward me. I reached for her and pulled her against me.

"Brady?" said Olivia.

"I understand," I said quietly. If Paul trailered his boat, he did not keep it moored at any marina. He kept it in his garage or driveway. Paul's boat would be in the water only if Paul was on it.

"I told them something happened," said Olivia. "He went out in that storm."

"I'm sure there's an explanation."

"I gave them your name," she said. "Was that all right?"

"Sure, Olivia. Anything I can do to help . . . "

"You *are* our lawyer."

"Yes, I am."

"So now what? Now what'm I supposed to do?"

"What did the Coast Guard tell you?"

"They said someone would be in touch. I guess they're . . . they're looking . . . "

"There's nothing else you can do," I said. "I'm sorry. It's hard. But all you can do is wait."

"He never wore a life jacket," she said. "He loved to go out alone at night. Especially when it was stormy. He said that a storm would churn up the bait, get the fish excited. It's so dumb."

"Hang in there, Olivia. Call me when—"

"When they find his body."

"Anytime. Call me when you hear anything. Or even if you don't. Whatever I can do to help, call me."

"Thank you," she said in a small voice. "Thank you, Brady."

I hung up the phone. Alex mumbled, "Everything okay?"

"No," I said. "Paul Cizek took his boat out this evening. The Coast Guard towed it in. Paul wasn't on it."

8

I lay there for awhile with Alex's cheek on my shoulder and her leg hooked over both of mine, but I couldn't get back to sleep. So I slid out from under her, pulled on my jeans and a clean T-shirt, and padded into the kitchen. I plugged in the coffee and leaned against the counter until it finished perking. Then I poured myself a mugful and took it out onto the balcony.

The storm had swept the air clean, and the sky was turning pink out on the eastern horizon. I didn't need a wristwatch to tell me that it was close to 5:00 A.M., because at that time of June the sun rises a little after five, and when I'm on my balcony I can see it happen.

Olivia Cizek, I figured, had called around four.

I imagined her sitting somewhere in her house sipping coffee and staring out the window waiting for the phone to ring. She and Paul had separated. But being separated wouldn't stop her from caring.

I remembered the last time I'd seen Paul. It had been at Glen Falconer's victory party. He'd asked for my help, and I'd tried to give it to him. But as far as I knew, he hadn't accepted it. Maybe I could have tried harder.

No. I'd done what I could. I was not responsible for his leaving Olivia.

The sun cracked the horizon on schedule, a sudden flare of light in the clear morning air. "Daybreak," it's called, and the word applies literally when it happens over the ocean.

It took only a few minutes for the earth to rotate far enough to reveal the entire circumference of the sun. The color quickly burned out of the sky, leaving it pale blue and cloudless. It promised to be a perfect Saturday in June.

Ideally I would spend a perfect June Saturday at a trout river. Mayflies of various species hatch from April through October on New England rivers, but their name is no coincidence. They hatch most prolifically in May and June—big, smoke-winged Hendricksons; March Browns and Gray Foxes, which look like miniature sailboats on the water with their barred wings unfurled; little yellow sulphurs and big yellow Light Cahills; and green drakes, which are really more cream-colored than green and look as big as sparrows when they lift off a river.

Mayflies are among Mother Nature's most graceful and beautiful creations, and I think I'd believe that even if trout didn't gluttonize on them when they ride on a stream's currents to dry their wings.

But trout do gluttonize on mayflies, and when they do, they can be fooled into eating an imitation made of feathers and fur and hair wound onto a small fishhook, provided, like the real thing, it drifts freely and naturally on the surface of the stream.

Selecting the best imitation to tie onto the end of my leader, casting it so that it drifts directly over a feeding trout, and doing it so cleverly that the trout confuses that fur-and-feather concoction with a real mayfly and pokes his nose out of the water to eat it— that is the appeal of trout fishing in June.

I figured I wouldn't do any fishing on this particular Saturday in June, keeping my nonfishing record for the season intact. Paul Cizek had gone overboard during the storm. Olivia would need me.

I was smoking a cigarette, working on my second mug of coffee, and watching the gulls cruise over the harbor when Alex kissed the back of my neck.

"Good morning, sweetie," she said.

I turned my head so she could kiss my cheek. Then I kissed hers. "Hi," I said. "Coffee's all brewed."

She showed me the mug she was holding. "Are you okay?"

"I'm pretty worried about Paul."

"Tell me about it. I was kind of out of it when the phone rang."

She sat in the aluminum chair beside me and held onto my hand while I talked. When I told her that Paul and Olivia had separated, she squeezed my hand a little harder.

"You think he went overboard during the storm," she said when I finished.

"I guess there are a lot of explanations for finding his boat out there without him on it," I said. "But that's the one that makes the most sense."

"If he went overboard—"

"He probably drowned. He never wore a life jacket. I'm trying not to create scenarios. There's nothing I can do about it. I'm just trying to wait and see what happens."

"His wife will call you again?"

"I expect so. If she doesn't, I'll call her."

"You were hoping to go fishing," she said.

"Yes. I was going to call Charlie and see if he wanted to go. If he didn't, I'd probably have gone alone. I haven't been all year. I've pretty much lost my heart for it now."

She lifted her mug, drained it, then stood up. "I've got to get to the office," she said. "Will you be okay?"

"Sure. It's Olivia I'm worried about."

Olivia called a little after eight. "They want to talk to me," she said.

"Who?"

"The Newburyport police."

"When?"

"As soon as I can get there."

"If you want," I said, "I can be in Newburyport in an hour."

"Oh, yes, thank you," she said softly. "I could really use your support." She was silent for a moment, then she said, "Brady?"

"Yes?"

"What do you think they want?"

"I guess they're just trying to figure out what might've happened."

"If they found him—his . . . his body—they would've told me, wouldn't they?"

"Yes, I think they would."

"So . . ."

"Try not to jump to conclusions, Olivia. Let's take it a step at a time. How well do you know Newburyport?"

"I've been there. Not well, I guess."

"When you turn off the highway onto Route 113 you'll see a Friendly's ice cream place on your left. I'll meet you there. We'll have a cup of coffee, then we can go talk to the police together. Okay?"

"Yes. Okay."

I hung up the phone and headed for the shower. The police wanted to question Olivia Cizek because they always want to question the spouse when someone dies mysteriously or violently.

The police were already assuming Paul Cizek had died.

Olivia may not have realized it, but she needed a lawyer.

I found her sitting at a booth staring into a cup of coffee. It didn't look as if she'd slept much.

I slid in across from her. "Good to see you again, Olivia."

She looked up and smiled quickly. "Thank you for coming," she said. She had pale gray eyes, almost silver, and a sprinkling of freckles across the bridge of her nose, and when she smiled the tiny lines at the corners of her eyes and her mouth crinkled.

I reached across the table and squeezed her hand. "It's a tough time for you. I'm your lawyer. And your friend."

"I'm a lawyer, too, you know."

I nodded.

"They think I might've done something," she said.

A waitress appeared at the table. "Just coffee, please," I said. "Bring the lady a refill." When she left, I said to Olivia, "You know how it works. You're the spouse. But I doubt if the police are pursuing any theories right now. They're investigating. They want all the information they can get. It's logical for them to talk to you, that's all."

"But you think you should be with me."

"Yes."

"To protect me."

"To protect your rights, yes. But mainly because I figured you could use a friend right now."

"I sure can. That's why I called you." She smiled quickly. "And I guess I understand that if that friend is also a lawyer, so much the better."

"So tell me about last night."

"What do you mean?"

"What you did."

She frowned, then said, "Oh. Like, do I have an alibi?"

I shrugged. "Yes."

"I had a meeting up in Salem until about seven-thirty or eight. Then I went home."

"Directly home?"

"Yes. Directly home."

"Then what?"

"Then nothing. I went home, heated a frozen chicken pie in the microwave, ate it while I watched the news on CNN, and went to bed. I read for a while and then went to sleep."

"Any phone calls?"

She frowned for a moment, then shook her head. "No. No calls. Nobody to verify where I was. That's what you're getting at, isn't it?"

"The police might ask," I said.

The waitress brought our coffees. Olivia stirred milk into hers.

"I don't have any alibi, Brady," she said. "After I left the meeting I went straight home. I had no visitors. I didn't talk to anybody on the phone until I got that call from the Coast Guard. I could've gone up to Newburyport and dumped Paul off his boat. There's nobody to say I didn't. Except me. And if you don't believe me—"

I gripped her wrist. "Stop," I said softly. "Cut it out. The police might ask these questions, and I want to know the answers before they do. No one's accusing you of anything." I let go of her wrist and took a sip of coffee. "It would help me to know what happened to the two of you."

She shrugged and looked down into her cup.

"You were separated," I said. "Paul moved out. What happened?"

She lifted her cup to her mouth and held it there for a moment. Then she put it down. "We just drifted apart, I guess."

"That's no answer, Olivia."

She looked at me, then nodded. "No. It's really not. It's true, but it's not really what happened. See, as soon as Paul took the job with Tarlin and Overton, he changed. Before, when he was prosecuting, he was a wild man. Just bubbling with energy and enthusiasm and—and righteous zeal. Oh, he loved to nail the bad guys. He was making justice happen, he liked to say. He really believed in it. He was like a kid. It was like electricity just crackled out of him. We had so much fun. I loved it. I thought he was the sexiest man. You know?"

I nodded. "I know what you mean," I said. "I knew Paul back then, too."

She took a quick sip of her coffee. "I mean, sometimes he'd work fourteen or sixteen hours a day. And when he got home he'd be absolutely wired. He'd keep me up half the night talking about his cases. We didn't see that much of each other. But when we were together, it was intense. I had my own career." She smiled. "Our life was full and complicated and exciting."

She bowed her head for a moment. When she looked up, she was no longer smiling. "Everything changed when he took that job. He still worked long hours, and he was making about ten times as much money. We bought a nice house and he got a new boat and everything, and we tried to pretend things were great. We were moving up in the world, right? But when he'd come home, he'd plop himself in front of the TV. Or during the fishing season he'd just change his clothes and hitch the trailer to his car and take off.

He didn't talk much about his work. When he did, all he'd say was that he was keeping bad guys out of prison. He didn't really complain about it, at least not at first. It took me a while to realize that he was trying to protect me. He didn't want to make me unhappy or to make me feel like he was suffering on account of me. But I knew he didn't believe in what he was doing. And he kept getting worse. He kept winning cases, and they'd reward him by giving him nastier people to defend. I mean, he had that child molester, and he had that Mafia man, and then he got that drunk driver—"

"I talked him into that one."

She shrugged. "It didn't matter. If it hadn't been that man, it'd've been someone else. The point is, gradually we just stopped talking. I finally started telling him he should quit and go back to work for the DA. He'd just smile. I tried to talk him into getting help. He was depressed, and I was worried about him."

"Did you ever think—?"

"He'd kill himself?" she said. "Is that what you think happened last night?"

"He's seemed awfully depressed to me last time I saw him."

She shook her head. "I don't know. He had his fishing. During the season, he seemed okay. Getting out on his boat alone at night always seemed to make him happy."

"He'd been worse lately, though?"

She smiled. "He never left me before."

I nodded.

"It was his idea, Brady. I didn't stop loving him or wanting to be with him. But he felt it was the only thing left to do. I don't know, maybe he thought it was just the only way left that would protect me. I never felt he didn't love me. But he was tortured, and he knew I was miserable. Even the fishing didn't help him anymore. He was desperate. I think part of it was that he put a lot of pressure on himself, trying to be admirable for me. He figured if he despised himself, I must despise him, too. I didn't. I loved him. But if we got divorced, he could stop worrying about how I felt about him. Does that make any sense?"

I shrugged. "I guess so. As much as anything makes sense." I took a sip of coffee, then said, "Did you ever go out on the boat with him?"

She frowned. "What . . . ? Oh. You mean, did I know how to operate it? Did I know his routines?"

"Yes."

"Could I have gone out with him last night, you mean."

I nodded.

"I could have. I mean, I've got nobody to say I didn't. But I didn't. But, yes, I went out with him a few times, especially . . . before. Before he changed jobs. It was sort of fun, but I knew he really liked it best when he was by himself. I could drive a boat, yes, and I could stun an eel and rig it on a line, and I knew how to read the currents and the tides and how to get a good drift through a rip. I didn't much care about the actual fishing. But I liked being on a boat with Paul at night. And I guess I could've been there last night, and I could've picked him up and thrown him overboard and then swam to shore and . . . "

I took both of her hands in mine. "Hey," I said softly.

"I know. I'm sorry, Brady."

"Just as long as you're telling me the truth."

She nodded. Tears brimmed in her eyes. "He's dead, isn't he?"

"I don't know. Let's talk to the police. Maybe they've learned something."

9

Olivia left her car in the Friendly's lot and rode with me into the business center of Newburyport. We parked in the municipal lot and headed for the police station. Newburyport, like most of the cities along the New England coastline, began as an old seafaring town because of its sheltered harbor. It was a fishing town and a trading town that grew and flourished inside the mouth of the Merrimack River. During the Industrial Revolution in the second half of the nineteenth century, factories were built along the riverbanks. Then, inevitably, the factories shut down and the merchant shipping industry faltered and Newburyport went through the predictable stages of decline.

During the past decade or two the city has been revitalized. The old factories have been converted into comtemporary office buildings and condominiums. The downtown area features brick-fronted shops that sell books and candles and chocolates and antiques. There are a dozen restaurants and taverns within a few blocks of each other, and all of them seem to be profitable.

Politically, Newburyport is a city. But it feels like a quaint old New England seaport town, just the way it's supposed to.

On this perfect Saturday morning in June, the twisting streets and the wide sidewalks were thronged with shoppers and tourists. Seagulls sailed overhead, and beyond the shops and restaurants the masts of schooners poked into the sky. The air tasted salty and clean.

"Where was Paul's house?" I asked Olivia as we crossed a brick-paved plaza.

"I don't know," she said. "Somewhere out on Plum Island."

"You've never been there?"

"No. He called it a shack. It's on some back road overlooking the marsh."

"He wouldn't let anybody borrow his boat?"

She laughed quickly. "Absolutely not."

"But he might've invited somebody along with him."

"Sure."

At the station, Olivia told the female desk cop that Lieutenant Kirschenbaum was expecting her, and a few minutes later a lanky, stoop-shouldered guy wearing a short-sleeved white shirt and baggy chino pants came out. "Mrs. Cizek?" he said.

"Yes. This is Mr. Coyne."

"Oh?" He had a thick mop of curly gray-blond hair. A pair of steel-rimmed glasses perched atop his head.

"He's my—our lawyer. Mine and Paul's."

Kirschenbaum looked at me and shrugged. "Sure, okay. You folks want to come on in here?"

He turned and slouched down a corridor, and we followed him into a small office. He folded himself into the swivel chair behind his desk, and Olivia and I took the straight-backed wooden chairs across from him.

Olivia put her forearms on the desk. "Do you know anything?"

"Nothing since we talked this morning," he said. "Someone radioed the Coast Guard that there was a boat adrift. That was around two in the morning. So they went out and towed it in. Nobody was aboard. They've got it at the Lifeboat Station on Water Street. There's a vehicle registered to Paul Cizek of Lynnfield parked at the public landing. It's got a boat trailer hooked to it." He poked at his hair, found his glasses, and placed them on the desk in front of him. "That's really all I can tell you. I was hoping you could shed some more light on it."

"You didn't find . . . ?"

He shook his head.

"I don't see how I can help you," she said.

"You two were, um, living apart."

She looked at him sharply. "Yes, we were. We separated at the end of March."

"Right," he said. He picked up his glasses and fitted them onto his ears, then rummaged around on his desk and found a manila folder. He opened it and bent to study the papers it held. Then he looked up at us. "He was renting the house at the end of Meadowridge Road, out on the island?"

She nodded. "That's right."

"He liked to fish," he said, still peering at the papers he was holding.

"He went out whenever he could. That's why when he moved out, he came up here. So he'd be near the ocean. He liked to go in the river and around Plum Island."

"And he fished at night?"

"Mostly at night, yes. He preferred to fish at night. He felt that's when the stripers bit the best. Anyway, he worked long hours during the day."

Kirschenbaum removed his glasses, folded them, and pointed them at Olivia. "He was pretty well known for defending some unsavory types."

"It's what he did."

"Yes. And he was very good at it, I understand. Was your husband suicidal, Mrs. Cizek?"

"Paul?" She frowned. "He was not happy. In fact, he's been quite depressed lately. But suicide?" She shook her head. "I don't think so. No. That wasn't Paul."

"Would you say he was a careful man?"

"What do you mean?"

"In his boat. Did he take risks?"

She shook her head. "I don't . . . "

"He never wore a life jacket," I said. "At least not when I was with him."

Kirschenbaum glanced at me, then turned back to Olivia. "There was a bad storm last night. We had big seas outside. Wind, heavy rain, lightning. Some pretty violent squalls. But he was out there in his boat."

"He had a lot of confidence in himself," she said. "He used to say that the fish bit best in the rain. He liked weather."

The cop turned to me. "Mr. Coyne, you were friends with Mr. Cizek, is that right?"

I nodded.

"Good friends?"

I shrugged. "Yes, I'd say we were good friends. We used to fish together. I was his family lawyer." I glanced at Olivia. She was peering at Kirschenbaum. "I did the Cizek's will and a few other legal odds and ends for them. Paul and I haven't been out fishing for a couple of years. We ran into each other now and then. Professionally, I mean. We threw business each other's way."

"You knew him pretty well, then?"

"I felt I knew him better a few years ago. Since he went private, we saw less of each other."

"What about recently?"

"I referred a client of mine to him, so I saw him several times this past fall and winter."

"That would be Falconer?"

"Yes. He defended Glen Falconer. Actually, Roger Falconer, Glen's father, is my client."

"And Mr. Cizek was successful in his defense of Mr. Falconer, as I remember."

I nodded.

"How did Cizek seem to you recently?"

"I haven't seen him since February. He was depressed. Confused."

Kirschenbaum arched his eyebrows.

"I recommended he get some counseling. I got some names for him, but I don't know if he ever followed up on it."

He turned to Olivia. "What about enemies, ma'am?"

She shrugged and looked at me.

"Lawyers make enemies," I said. "Paul had high-profile cases. He defended people who were accused of serious crimes, and he was often successful. There are always victims of serious crimes. He was threatened in court last winter. The husband of the woman who was killed by the drunk driver Paul defended."

Kirschenbaum nodded. "I remember hearing about that." He turned to Olivia. "Where were you last night, Mrs. Cizek?"

Olivia glanced at me, then turned to Kirschenbaum and smiled quickly. "After about eight o'clock, I don't have an alibi."

"Oh, I wasn't looking for an alibi," he said with a wave of his hand. "I was just wondering where you were."

"Home alone."

"When was the last time you talked to your husband?"

"A few days ago. Wednesday, I think it was. We talked on the phone for about an hour that evening. We were working out the terms of our separation."

"How did your husband seem?"

"Stressed out. Sad. Depressed."

"Did you argue?"

"No. We never argued. In all the time we've known each other, we haven't argued."

Kirschenbaum leaned forward. "Mrs. Cizek, I want to ask you a hard question."

She nodded. "All right."

"Was your husband involved with somebody else?"

"A woman, you mean?"

He spread his hands.

"I don't think so," she said.

"Then that's not what caused . . . ?"

"Our separation?" She shrugged. "No. Not as far as I know." She shook her head. "I don't know. Maybe. He'd grown awfully distant over the past couple of years."

"What about you?"

"Me?"

"Were you—"

"No. I wasn't involved with anybody. I was still involved with Paul."

Kirschenbaum glanced at his papers for a moment, then took off his glasses and stuck them on top of his head. "I guess you understand what we're looking at here," he said to Olivia.

"You think Paul's dead," she said.

He glanced at me, then nodded. "It's the logical assumption. The Coast Guard is searching for a body. The problem is, we don't know where he was when he—if he went over. The tide was running, there were heavy winds, we don't know how long the boat had been adrift before it was spotted. A few boats broke away from their moorings in the storm last night. But your husband trailered his, so that's out. He's not at his house. You haven't heard from him." He flapped his hands. "We try not to jump to conclusions, but . . . "

Olivia nodded. I could see her jaw muscles bunch and clench. "You'll keep me informed?" she said in a low voice.

"Of course," said Kirschenbaum. "And if you hear anything, you'll tell me."

"Yes."

"You too, Mr. Coyne."

"Sure," I said.

"You'll be available, then?" he said to Olivia.

"Don't leave town, right?" she said, trying to smile.

"I've got your number," he said.

Outside the police station, Olivia stopped, turned to me, and pressed her face against my chest. I put my arms around her and held her against me.

"I tried to keep it together in there," she mumbled.

"You did fine," I said.

"I don't know what to do."

"We can only wait."

"That's the hardest thing."

I patted her shoulders. "I know."

10

I fully agreed with Olivia. Waiting is hard. It's always better to do something, no matter what it is.

I drove her back to the Friendly's parking lot and gave her a hug. She climbed into her red Saab, and I waved to her as she headed home to Lynnfield. Then I turned around and drove back into Newburyport.

On my first try I went right past the Cashman Park boat ramp, the municipal launch area. I'd met Paul there a few times for fishing excursions, but that had been a couple of years earlier and at night. I remembered it was just before you cross Route 1 into town, so I turned around, drove back along the narrow street that paralleled the river, and found the entrance tucked alongside a big brick factory building.

The parking area was crowded with vehicles on this Saturday noon in June. Most of them had boat trailers attached. I found a slot near the entrance, wedged into it, and climbed out of my car.

I meandered down to the concrete ramp that slanted into the Merrimack. An elderly guy wearing baggy blue shorts and a plain white T-shirt was taking money from a young couple who were launching a small motorboat.

When they finished their transaction, I approached the man. He was wearing a cap that advertised Surfland Bait & Tackle. Tufts of white hair poked out from under it. "Excuse me," I said.

He turned to me, and I saw that his sun-browned face was patched with large, irregularly shaped freckles. "Hiya," he said. "You launching?"

"No. Can I ask you a couple questions?"

He shrugged. "About what?"

"Do you know Paul Cizek?"

He cocked his head and squinted at me. "Who're you?"

"I'm Paul's lawyer."

He nodded as if that made perfect sense. "Cops was already here. I told 'em everything."

"Did you see Paul last night?"

He smiled, and a maze of wrinkles spread over his face like a sudden breeze on a glassy pond. "Cops asked that. Told 'em I got off at seven. Mr. Cizek, he usually launches later, just around sunset. Night fisherman. He's got a season pass, see, so he don't need to do business with me. And usually he takes out before I get here in the morning. I bump into him once in a while. Usually, he's in and out when I'm not here." He shrugged. "I didn't see him last night. Nope."

"So you wouldn't know if he had anybody with him."

He shook his head. "Usually when I see him he's alone. Except for the fish. Often as not, he brings a keeper back with him. Good fisherman, Mr. Cizek. He can find 'em. Guess something happened to him, huh?"

I nodded. "The Coast Guard found his boat last night. He wasn't on it."

"Wish I could help you," he said. "Nice guy, Mr. Cizek. Friendly, you know? Treats a man like a man, if you understand me. Not like some of 'em." He jerked his shoulder at the parked cars. "I mean, I s'pose I'm just the guy they give their money to. But still . . . "

"Mr.—" I began.

"Randolph," he said.

"Mr. Randolph—"

"No, no," he said, shaking his head. "Randolph's my first name. They call me Dolph, mostly."

I held out my hand. "I'm Brady. That's my first name, too." We shook hands. "Dolph," I said, "I'm trying to figure out what happened last night."

"I sure don't know."

"What do you think?"

"Me?" He smiled. "Cops didn't ask me that. Guess they didn't figure I could think." He jabbed his forefinger at my shoulder. "Tell you what, though. They think Mr. Cizek went over in the storm. I don't buy it. Not him. Not in that Whaler of his. No, sir."

"Why not?"

"Mr. Cizek's a good sailor. Knows this river, knows the tides, knows how the winds work. He goes out last night, he knows where to go. Big seas like that, he's got his spots. Night like we had, he knows the bait gets blowed close to shore, in on the beaches, near the rocks. He fishes in weather all the time. Ain't gone over before, no reason he would last night." He paused. "Tell you what else. Say something did happen. What'd happen would be, he gets blowed onto the rocks, maybe, or onto some beach. See, that's where Mr. Cizek'd be. Where the bait is, which is where the fish are. Where'd they find that Whaler of his?"

"Adrift," I said. "Out past Plum Island."

Randolph shook his head. "Don't make sense. He wouldn't of been fishin' outside. He'd of been inside, workin' the rocks and jetties. Was it bunged up?"

"Huh?"

"You know. The boat. Was it bunged up? Like it got blowed against the rocks."

"I don't know."

"You might maybe want to find out."

I nodded. "Good idea."

"I don't buy it," he said again. "Not Mr. Cizek."

He pointed out Paul's car, a Jeep Cherokee with a trailer hitched behind it, and I went over and looked at it. But I didn't see anything that told me what had happened that night.

So I waved at Randolph, climbed back into my car, and drove through town and out Water Street to the Coast Guard station. I found a parking spot across the street. A long, double-wide driveway led past a hangar-shaped garage down to the water, and I followed it, half expecting to be halted by an armed sentry. But nobody seemed to notice me.

On the left was what I took to be the administration building, a low, rambling structure with a well-manicured lawn and flower gardens ablaze with marigolds and impatiens. Out back on a basketball court a gang of young men in shorts and T-shirts were playing volleyball. There were lots of shouts and curses and good-natured laughter, and I stopped to watch. They played with vast youthful energy and enthusiasm. One young fellow with a blond ponytail dove for a spectacular save, and I figured he'd have scabby knees for a month.

When he stood up, his teammates slapped his bottom, and I saw that he was a woman. In fact, several of the players were women.

None of them took notice of me, so I wandered down to the water. Half a dozen Coast Guard vessels of various sizes and configurations were moored there, along with a few other boats.

One was a Boston Whaler. I moved out onto the end of the short dock and read *Olivia* on her transom. From what I could see, she had not been bunged up at all.

I looked around, but still nobody seemed to be paying any attention to me. So I sat on the edge of the dock and slid aboard *Olivia*.

She was a sixteen- or seventeen-footer, with a center console, no cabin, shallow draft. A good boat to fish from, broad-beamed, high-sided, and open, but not made for the high seas. A tall antenna poked up from the console, and I remembered fly casting from the bow in the wind and snagging my line on it. Sure. *Olivia* had a radio, so if Paul had been in trouble, he'd have called for help. But Lieutenant Kirschenbaum hadn't mentioned any Mayday call from Paul, so I assumed he'd made none.

Whatever happened had happened suddenly and without warning.

I looked around the inside of the boat. Shipshape, the way Paul liked it. The rods with both level-wind and spinning reels were racked neatly in their holders along the gunwales. The lines were coiled and the bumpers stowed. I lifted the lid of the built-in bait box at the stern, but it was empty. So was the fish box beside it. I lifted the hatch in the bow and counted the life jackets. There were four, which was the number he always carried.

I went back to the console. I noticed that the key was in the ignition. The dry storage at its base was empty. It's where Paul always kept his tackle box.

I sat on the seat behind the wheel and lit a cigarette. No bait, no tackle box. It was puzzling.

"Can I help you, sir?"

I looked up. It was the ponytailed volleyball player.

"How can you do that without skinning your knees?" I said.

She frowned. She looked to be about Billy's age. My older son had just turned twenty-one. "Pardon me?" she said.

"The way you were diving on the court for the ball."

She smiled. "You've gotta know how to do it." She hesitated. "You're not supposed to be here. This isn't your boat, is it?"

"No. It belongs to a friend of mine."

"You better come up." She held her hand down to me. I took it and she helped me climb back onto the dock. "They brought her in last night some time," she said. "Found her adrift."

"I know. My friend was probably on it."

"Oh, geez," she said. "I thought it had just busted a mooring or something."

"No," I said. "It was launched from a trailer. I'm just trying to figure out what might've happened."

"One of the guys was talking about it," she said. "They got a call a little after midnight. Someone spotted her with nobody aboard. So they went out and brought her in. She was just the way she is now. Ignition and radio both off. No anchor over the side."

"And no bait and no tackle box."

She cocked her head. "So?"

"My friend used her for fishing. He's a bait fisherman. He wouldn't go out without some eels or bunker or whatever the bait of the hour might be. He always brought bait with him."

She shrugged. "Maybe he didn't last night. Maybe he was casting plugs or something. Maybe he was drift-fishing, so the engine was turned off, and he was leaning over or casting or something, you know, off balance, and a swell caught him and just flipped him out. He wouldn't've had a chance to use the radio if it happened like that."

"No tackle box, either," I said.

"It could've gone over, too. It was pretty choppy out there last night." She shook her head. "But, you know—"

At that moment, someone yelled, "Hey, Morrison! What in hell're you doing?"

The girl's cheeks reddened as she turned to face a man of about my age stalking rapidly toward us. He wore creased chino pants and a white polo shirt. When he got closer, I saw the Coast Guard insignia stitched on the shirt pocket.

"We were examining the craft, sir," she said.

"She was telling me I had to move away from it," I said.

He looked from Morrison to me, then back to her. Curly black hair matted his head and forearms and crawled out of his shirt at the throat. His shoulders and chest bulged. "Okay," he said after a moment. "Good work, Ensign. Dismissed."

"Yes, sir," she said, snapping him a quick salute. She started to leave, then turned to me. "I hope it works out okay with your friend," she said.

"Thank you. And you take care of your knees."

She grinned quickly, then headed back to the volleyball court.

"The police want us to keep people away from this boat," the man said to me.

"I didn't know," I said. "But that's what Ensign Morrison was telling me. She spoke very sternly to me."

He nodded. "I bet she did."

"This is Paul Cizek's boat," I said. "I'm his lawyer. He launched it from the municipal ramp last night sometime. It looks as if something happened to him."

"Looks that way," he said. "But I can't help you."

"I was wondering," I said. "Was there any bait in the bait box when you brought her in?"

He frowned. "Bait?"

"You know. Eels, menhaden, squid."

"I know what bait is," he said. "All I can tell you is that nobody's touched anything on that boat."

"I just thought if the bait box had bait in it . . . "

"Yeah," he said. "It'd stink up the place. But nobody cleaned it up, if that's what you were getting at. This is how she was when we found her. Look. I probably shouldn't have even told you that. It's a local police matter. You want to talk to anybody, talk to them."

I nodded. "Good advice. Thanks."

"I'll walk you out," he said, and I figured if I balked he'd carry me out.

"I think I can find my way," I said. "Thanks anyway."

When I got to the end of the driveway, I glanced back. He was standing there with his arms folded over his chest, watching me. I waved. He lifted one hand quickly, then turned away. I crossed the street and climbed into my car.

11

I went to The Grog, my favorite Newburyport hangout, and found an empty stool at the end of the bar. I ordered a draft beer and a cheeseburger, then sat there with my chin on my fist trying to imagine what might've happened to Paul.

I thought the obvious thoughts: A sudden gust of wind or a swell hitting the boat from the wrong angle had knocked him off balance and tumbled him overboard; he had gone voluntarily into the sea, a suicide; or, some enemy had managed to kill him and throw him to the ocean's scavengers.

I also considered the possibility that Paul had set it up, faking his death. Except the only people I'd ever heard of doing that were fugitives or life-insurance scammers, and Paul was neither of those. Anyway, he loved his boat too much to set it adrift in a storm.

The police evidently were leaning to the accident scenario, and for good reason. There are many more accidents at sea than suicides or murders or sham disappearances. The commonest things most commonly happen, they believe, and in the absence of evidence to the contrary, that is the theory they generally pursue.

I believe that, too. Except the absence of bait on *Olivia* made me doubt that Paul had ventured out to catch a striped bass, and if he hadn't gone fishing, there was no reason for him to have gone out in that storm at all.

Suicide? He'd been depressed, profoundly discontent with his work. His marriage was in the process of dissolving. Middle-aged angst. Midlife crisis. I understood the feelings. Most of my friends had them, and I certainly was not immune to them. But neither I nor any of my friends killed ourselves because we were starting to ask questions such as Is this all there is? and What's it all about, anyway?

That left murder. Paul Cizek, like most of us, had enemies, perhaps even people angry enough to want to kill him. I figured Lieutenant Kirschenbaum had probably considered that possibility, even if it wasn't the commonest thing. I had trouble imagining Paul Cizek being murdered. I had trouble imagining murder, period. It happened on the news. But it didn't happen to my friends.

When they found his body, they'd know. And if they never found his body, they never would know.

I ate my burger and drank my beer, then found the pay phone. Olivia answered in the middle of the first ring.

"It's Brady," I said.

"Oh, gee," she said. "Have you heard anything?"

"No. I—"

"When the phone rang, I was hoping . . . "

"I'm sorry. It's just me. I'm still here in Newburyport. You've had no news, either, then?"

"No. Nothing."

"Are you okay?"

She laughed quickly. "Okay? Well, no, I'm not okay at all. I'm having a lot of trouble with this, as a matter of fact. I'm sitting here staring at the telephone, trying to make it ring and for it to be Paul, telling me he's fine. And so far it isn't working." She hesitated. "You're in Newburyport?"

"Yes. I decided to poke around a little while I was here."

"Did you learn anything at all?"

I told her about my chat with Randolph and my visit to the Coast Guard station.

"What do you make of it?" she said. "He never went out without bait."

"It makes the accident scenario less likely, I guess," I said. "Otherwise, I don't know." I paused. "Olivia, did Paul have a lot of life insurance?"

"Oh, geez," she said. Then she laughed quickly. "You're thinking he—"

"It's a thought."

"He had a couple of small policies. Just enough to get himself buried, he liked to say. He figured he could take care of me better by investing."

"I just wondered," I said lamely.

She said nothing. Finally I said, "Are you there, Olivia?"

"I'm here," she said. "I was just thinking . . . "

"What?"

"That you're a nice man to—to care."

"Paul is my friend. So are you."

"You don't have to do this, Brady."

"It makes me feel better to be doing something."

"I wish *I* could do something."

"You guard that telephone. I'm sure you'll hear something soon."

"Are you?"

"Am I what?"

"Are you sure?"

"No, I guess not." I shifted the phone to my other ear, then said, "Do you know where his house is?"

"Paul's?"

"Yes."

"I've never been there, but he told me about it. It's on, um, Meadowridge Road, or Street, or something. On the island. When you cross the bridge, you go left, I remember him saying that, because if you turn right you go into the wildlife sanctuary. It's overlooking the marsh. He told me about all the ducks he could see from his windows. Why, Brady?"

"I thought I'd go out and take a look."

"You don't need to do this," she said softly.

"I'm right here. It'll make me feel useful."

"Well, that's nice. Let me know what you find, okay?"

"You can count on it."

So I got into my car and headed back out Water Street, past the Coast Guard station, and along the Merrimack River, and I kept following the river until I crossed the bridge and found myself on Plum Island. I turned left onto the narrow street. It was half covered with wind-blown sand, and it ran between the island's dunes on the right and the salt marsh bordering the river on the left. It was lined on both sides with closely packed summer cottages of every architectural description except "elegant." They looked cramped and run-down, the sorts of places that stay in families for generations of progressively accumulating neglect.

The yards were tiny and sandy, featuring tufts of marsh grass and plastic ride toys and clotheslines flapping with underwear and bathing suits and towels, and every hundred feet or so a little unpaved road bisected the street I was on, and along both sides of each side street were more ramshackle cottages.

I drove slowly, examining the road signs, and after about half a mile I spotted Meadowridge on the left. I pulled onto the sandy shoulder, turned off the ignition, and climbed out.

An insistent breeze blew directly down the street I had been traveling, and it tasted salty and peppered my bare arms and face with tiny grains of sand. I crossed quickly and started down Meadowridge. It was a short street—a couple of hundred feet long, at most—and I could see the marsh down at the end. Four cottages were lined up on each side, all of more or less similar design and set back precisely the same distance from the single-lane, packed-sand roadway.

An ancient yellow Volkswagen beetle was parked in the short driveway of the last cottage on the left. On the rear bumper was a sticker that read, JUST SAY YO.

I spotted a woman kneeling at a flower bed by the front steps. Her back was to me, so I approached to a distance from which I could speak to her without either startling her or invading her space. I cleared my throat, then said, "Excuse me?"

She turned her head, still kneeling. She looked like a teenager, although I have trouble judging the ages of young women. She wore dirty cotton gloves, and one hand held a trowel. She pointed the trowel at me and said, "Are you talking to me?"

"Yes. I'm sorry to bother you. I'm looking for Paul Cizek's house."

She sat back on her haunches and wiped her forehead with the back of her glove. She had blond hair held back with a rubber band, but wisps had gotten loose and she thrust out her lower lip and blew them away from her face. Then she frowned at me. "Who're you?"

"I'm a friend of Paul's."

"He's not home now."

"I know."

"Then—"

"Can you just tell me where he lives, Miss?"

She looked at me for a minute, then shook her head. "Sorry." She turned back and resumed troweling.

I took a few steps closer to her. "I know he lives on this street," I said. "I'm his lawyer."

"He's his own lawyer, far as I know," she mumbled without turning around.

"No. I'm his lawyer. We lawyers hire other lawyers to do our personal legal work for us. We say any lawyer who tries to do it himself has a fool for a lawyer. Lots of people say anyone who hires a lawyer has hired a fool."

I heard her chuckle, but she kept her back to me and didn't respond.

"Paul's boat was found adrift last night," I said. "He wasn't on it."

She turned. Her eyes bored into mine. They were green, almost the identical color of Alex's eyes. "What'd you say?" she said.

"Paul Cizek seems to be missing. The Coast Guard towed his boat in last night."

She stood up and came toward me. She was tall and lanky in her dirt-smeared T-shirt and snug running shorts. "You got some kind of identification, Mister?"

I fished a card from my wallet and held it out to her. She shucked off her gloves, tucked them into her armpit, took my card, and squinted at it. Then she looked up at me. "I still don't know what you want," she said.

I shrugged. "I don't honestly know myself. I've talked to the police, I've talked to the Coast Guard, and I've even talked to the guy at the boat launch. I'm just trying to figure out what happened to Paul. I thought I'd take a look at where he lived. I don't know what I expect to find, but—"

"He lives here."

"Here?"

"This is his place. I'm planting some flowers for him. It's kind of a surprise."

"Why?"

"He's—we're friends. I thought some petunias might cheer him up."

"Have you seen him today?"

"No. Listen. He's not missing."

"He's not?"

She smiled quickly. "Not Paul. There's a mistake. It's gotta be somebody else's boat they found. He'd never—"

"It's his boat," I said. "I saw it."

She stared at me. Then I saw the tears well up in her eyes. "Aw, shit," she said. "That bastard."

"Who?"

"Paul. That asshole. He did it, didn't he?"

"Did what?"

"He fucking killed himself." She made a fist and punched her thigh. "Son of a *bitch!*"

I reached out and touched her arm. "Can we talk?"

She narrowed her eyes. Tears streaked the dirt on her face. After a minute, she nodded. "Sure. We can talk. Come on."

I followed her onto the narrow deck that stretched across the back of the house. She lifted a flowerpot, removed a key, unlocked the door, then replaced the key. "Why don't you have a seat," she said, gesturing at a pair of wooden deck chairs. "I'll get us some iced tea. Okay?"

"That'd be fine," I said.

I sat in one of the chairs and lit a cigarette. Beyond a rim of low sand dunes lay a broad expanse of tall marsh grass. The tide was high, and little channels and creeks flowed through the marsh to the Merrimack half a mile away. A pair of black ducks skidded into a pothole in the grass, and seagulls wheeled in the breeze.

It struck me as a good place to sit and look and think, like my balcony over the harbor. I wondered how much time Paul had spent out here, sitting and looking and thinking.

The young woman came out a couple of minutes later carrying a pair of plastic glasses. "I'm Maddy Wilkins, by the way," she said. She handed me a glass. "I live a couple of streets down."

"Oh. I wondered . . . "

"If I was living with him?"

I nodded.

"I'm not, no. Not yet, anyway." She gestured at the glass I was holding. "Sun tea," she said. "I made it."

I took a sip. It tasted bitter.

"So you and Paul are—"

"Are what?"

I shrugged. "Lovers?"

She smiled. "That's a funny, old-fashioned word, isn't it?"

"Whatever."

"I don't see how that's any of your business," she said.

"He's married, you know."

"Yeah, I know that. So what? He's getting a divorce." She cocked her head. "I get it. You're his lawyer. The divorce, right?"

"They hadn't gotten that far, I guess. I wasn't representing him on it, anyway. I did other lawyer work for him. Him and his wife."

"So you know her, too, huh?"

"Yes."

She took the chair beside me. "Is he really missing?"

"Yes."

"They haven't—"

"They found his boat. Nobody knows what happened. You seem to think he might have taken his own life."

She hugged herself. "I don't know. He was always so sad. Except when he went fishing. Then he was a different man. But mostly he was just sad."

"Did he talk to you about it?"

"No, not really. He tried to act cheerful for me. But he wasn't very good at it. I'd come over, make supper for him, and we'd sit out on the deck and hold hands and watch the sun set over the marsh and all the ducks coming in, and he'd just stare into space, and . . . it was just *so* damn sad. I would've done anything to cheer him up. I tried every way I knew." She shook her head. "That's why I was planting those stupid petunias. Aw, shit." She tried to smile as the tears coursed down her cheeks. "My mother was right. If you don't love somebody, you can't get hurt. Damn it."

"Maddy," I said softly, "did he ever take you out on his boat?"

She nodded. "Sure. Boy, did he know how to find those fish."

"How did he catch them?"

"Eels, mostly. He'd either drift them or rig them and cast them. He loved eels. I never saw him fish any other way. He said later when the pogies started running he'd use them. But they haven't started yet."

"Did you see Paul yesterday?"

She shook her head. "I worked till eleven. I'm waitressing at Scandia. I'm in college, see, but we're done for the summer. So me and some girls've rented this place a couple streets down. Anyway, I came over when I got off, but he wasn't here. I figured he was fishing, even though it was wicked stormy."

"Did it surprise you that he'd go out in the storm?"

"Not at all. He went out in worse weather than that. I mean, I've been out with him in some pretty bad weather. We never had a problem. He'd stick close to land, and he was real careful. Always made me wear a life jacket."

"Did he wear one?"

She shook her head. "He said if you respected the sea and understood it, you'd never have a problem."

I sat there with Maddy Wilkins, sipping her bitter tea and trying to decide what else I might ask her. But I had run out of questions.

So I put down my half-empty glass, stood up, and said, "Thank you, Maddy."

She looked up and frowned. "For what?"

I shrugged. "For the tea. For the information. I hope you'll keep my card, and if you think of something or hear something you'll call me."

"Oh, sure. Okay."

She followed me off the deck and around to the front of Paul's little house. "Well," she said, "I might as well finish planting these petunias. For—for when he comes home."

"I'm sure he'll be cheered by them," I said.

We waved to each other and I started down Meadowridge Road to my parked car, and that's when I saw the big man with the black beard.

12

He was standing in the middle of the narrow sand road, about fifty feet from me, wearing blue jeans and a sleeveless muscle shirt and dark glasses. It looked as if he was staring at me from behind those glasses, but I couldn't see his eyes.

He looked familiar. I couldn't place him.

I started toward him, and he turned and walked briskly away, heading back to the main street.

Then I remembered. I had seen him with his fist shaking in the air and anger cut into his face. Thomas Gall. He had been shouting above the tumult in the courtroom, spitting threats at Glen Falconer and the judge and the jury. And at Paul Cizek.

"Hey," I called. "Hey, wait a minute."

He didn't turn. I started to jog after him as he disappeared around the corner.

When I got to the end of Meadowridge Road, I looked in the direction he had gone. A hundred yards or so down the street a dark pickup truck started up and pulled away from the side of the road, heading back toward the bridge that crossed the river into Newburyport.

I stood there watching the truck disappear down the street.

"Do you know that man?"

I turned. Maddy Wilkins was standing behind me.

"I know who he is," I said. "Did you recognize him?"

She tucked a long strand of blond hair behind her ear. "Sure. He's a friend of Paul's."

"A friend?"

"I guess so. I've seen him a few times. I came over one night and they were sitting out on Paul's deck."

"What were they doing?"

She shook her head. "I'd just gotten out of work—it must've been close to midnight—and I saw his lights on, so I thought I'd drop in and say hello. When I saw Paul had company, I turned around and left."

"You've seen him more than once, though, huh?"

"A couple times I noticed him sort of hanging around when Paul wasn't here. Kinda like he was doing today. I never talked to the man or anything." She frowned at me. "Is there some problem with him?"

"I don't know," I said. "Maybe."

I took Route 1A, the slow road, back toward Boston. It crossed tidal creeks and meandered past marshland and farmland and woods and passed through quiet little New England towns like Newbury and Rowley, with white Protestant churches and white eighteenth-century colonials perched on the rims of emerald village greens. I bore left on 133 in Ipswich and headed out toward Cape Ann, and in Essex I stopped at a seafood shanty and bought a quart of mussels and a couple of fresh tuna steaks. I picked up 128 in Gloucester and headed home.

It was nearly five in the afternoon when I got back to my apartment. I made room for the mussels and fish by removing a bottle of Samuel Adams from the refrigerator. Then Sam and I wandered into the living room. The red light on my answering machine indicated that three people had tried to call me—or that one person had tried three times, maybe.

Nope. Three people. The first was Alex, asking what our plan was. The second was Olivia, requesting that I call her.

The third was Gloria, my ex-wife. "Have you talked to Joseph?" her recorded voice said. "You better give me a call."

That sounded ominous, so I sat down, lit a cigarette, and dialed the Wellesley number that was still familiar more than a decade after it had been mine.

She answered after several rings. "Yes?" She sounded breathless.

"Are you all right?" I said.

"Oh, Brady." I heard her let out a long breath. "Yes, I'm fine. I was just getting out of the shower."

"What's the matter with Joey?"

"Joseph?" She hesitated. "Oh. My message. Nothing's the matter. Did I say something was the matter?"

"Not exactly. You asked if I'd talked to him. It sounded like—"

"I didn't mean to upset you, Brady. Sometimes Joseph tells me things that he doesn't tell you, and sometimes it's vice versa, and sometimes he tells us both, and sometimes he gives each of us different stories. William mainly talks to you, I know. But with Joseph, you never can tell."

"I haven't talked to Joey in a while," I said.

"You don't know that he's coming home, then."

"No. When?"

"Tonight, actually."

"Well, great. It'll be terrific to see him."

"The thing is," said Gloria, "I'm picking him up at the airport tonight and he's got to be in Chatham tomorrow for his job."

"His job?"

"He's got a job at a restaurant. He starts tomorrow afternoon."

"Well, shit," I said. "He didn't tell me any of this. So I don't even get to see him."

"I guess the job was sort of a last-minute thing," she said. "Anyway, I wondered if you might like to meet him at the airport with me. You and Alex, I mean. We could have coffee or something."

"Absolutely. What time?"

"Eleven-twenty at United. He's spent the past week visiting with his brother, and he's coming in from Boise. I told him I'd meet him at the baggage claim."

"We'll be there," I said. "And Gloria?"

"Yes?"

"Thank you. You didn't have to do this."

"You'd have done the same if the situation were reversed," she said.

"I hope I would," I said.

After Gloria and I disconnected, I called the *Globe* and, at the command of the recorded voice, punched in Alex's extension.

"Alexandria Shaw," she said.

"Rearranging verbs?"

"Oh, hi, sweetie. No, right now I'm trying to lose a hundred words. Golden words, these. It seems uncuttable."

"I assume you're coming over afterwards."

"Absolutely. I propose a game of strip Trivial Pursuit on the living room floor."

"Wouldn't seem right," I said, "you being naked and me fully dressed."

"It hardly ever works out that way, if you've noticed."

"It's just that I hate to see a woman take off her clothes alone. I take off my clothes out of a sense of good fellowship. Anyway, before our contest of wits, we're going to the airport. Joey's flying in tonight."

"That's fine. Is he going to stay with you?"

"No. Gloria's going to be there, too. She's taking him down to the Cape tomorrow for his summer job. This'll be my only chance to see him."

Alex chuckled. "So I get to meet your son and your ex-wife all at the same time."

"You don't have to come. I mean, if you think it'll be awkward . . . "

"Don't you want me to?"

"I do. I hope you will."

"I'd like to. Let me clean things up here. I'll be there in an hour or so."

"I'll cook something."

"Good. I'm starving."

"Any buzz on Paul Cizek at the paper?"

"Not really. Can you talk about it?"

"Sure. When you get here."

Alex made kissing noises into the phone, and we disconnected. Then I called Olivia.

"Yes?" she answered.

"It's Brady."

"Oh, gee. Thanks for calling back. I just . . . I wanted to hear a friendly voice."

"No news, then?"

"Nothing. Not a word. I tried calling Lieutenant Kirschenbaum, but he wasn't there. Nobody would tell me anything."

"If they knew something, I think they'd tell you."

"I guess so. You haven't heard anything, either?"

"No." I hesitated, then said, "I went out to Paul's house and talked to somebody, but she didn't know anything."

"She?"

"Just one of Paul's neighbors," I said.

"Well," she said, "I guess we can only wait." She hesitated for a moment, then said, "Brady?"

"Yes?"

"You *are* my attorney here, aren't you?"

"I don't think you need an attorney, Olivia."

"I want to retain you."

"It's not necessary."

"I'd like you to help me figure out what happened, Brady. Help me deal with it. I'd feel better if it was businesslike."

"Fine, Olivia. If that's how you'd prefer it. I'll have Julie work up an agreement on Monday."

"Thank you," she said. "We'll stay in touch, okay?"

"Okay."

I hung up and wandered out onto my balcony with my bottle of beer. We were approaching the longest day of the year, and the sun's rays still beat down on the harbor from a high angle. A brisk breeze riffled the water, and gulls and terns were wheeling and cruising sideways, riding on air currents.

Olivia had hired herself an attorney. I wondered if there was anything she wasn't telling me.

I was at the kitchen sink scrubbing the sand and grit off the mussels with a stiff-bristled brush when I heard Alex's key in the door. A moment later her arms went around my waist and she was pressing herself against my back.

"Hey, babe," she whispered into my shoulder.

"Hey, yourself."

"Sorry I'm late. I needed to go over some things with Michael."

"Good old Michael."

She turned me around, held me by the hips, and leaned back so that her lower half was pressed against my lower half. She was grinning. "Are we jealous of Michael?"

"Not we," I said. "Me."

"Of Michael?"

"Sure. He commands meetings when you should be with me."

She went up on tiptoes and kissed me on the ear. "Actually," she said, "it was I who requested the meeting."

"While I slave over the kitchen sink."

"You're cute in your little apron." She wrapped her arms around my chest and tucked her head up under my chin. "What're you making?"

"Mussles steamed in wine and garlic, tuna steaks grilled on the hibachi with butter and lemon, baked new potatoes, tossed salad, a bottle of chilled Marques de Caceres Rioja." I stepped out of her embrace, took off my apron, and reached for her hand. "Come with me, woman."

She smiled. "Yes, sir."

I led her into the living room. "Sit," I commanded, and she sat on the sofa. I sat on the coffee table in front of her, lifted her feet onto my lap, and slid off her shoes. Then I set about massaging her feet, giving each toe the careful, individual attention it deserved.

Alex leaned back and closed her eyes. "Oh, my God," she groaned. "I think I'm gonna come."

I rubbed her ankles and kneaded the hard muscles of her calves.

Her skin was smooth and warm to my touch. "I like it best in the summer," I said, watching her face, "when you don't wear panty hose."

She opened her eyes and looked at me. "Brady?"

"Mmm?"

"Stop. Now."

"You don't like it?"

"I *love* it. Now stop. Right this minute."

"Oh, I get it."

She sat up, put her arms around my neck, and kissed me hard. "Are you really jealous of Michael?" she whispered.

"I'm jealous of every man, because I know what they're thinking when they see you."

"How do you know what they're thinking?"

"Because I know what *I'm* thinking when *I* see you."

"That's awfully sweet." She kissed me again, then pulled back. "Can we eat? I'm starved."

I tried to look hurt. "I was planning to work my way up past your knees and under your skirt."

"Just how far were you planning to go?"

"I hadn't really decided where I'd stop. I just wanted to relax you after your long Saturday at the office."

"Relax?"

"Isn't it relaxing?"

She smiled. "Hardly. Anyway, we shouldn't get into that yet. We might lose track of time and not make it to the airport."

I mixed a rum and tonic for Alex and forbade her from helping. I steamed the mussels and dumped them into a big bowl, and we ate them at the table by the sliding doors, shelling them and dipping them in their own broth, while the potatoes baked in the oven and the sky darkened over the harbor. Then I tossed the salad and grilled the tuna.

By the time we cleaned up the kitchen, the moon had risen and the stars had begun to wink. We sat out on the balcony with our coffee and watched the reflections play on the water.

"Tell me about your day," Alex said.

So I did, ending with my conversation with Olivia.

"She hired you?"

"Yes."

"What for?"

"I'm not sure. To help, she said. I think she just wants support. She's feeling alone and frightened."

"Should I be jealous?"

I reached for her hand and squeezed it. "Olivia is rather attractive, actually, in a reserved, British sort of way. I'd prefer it if you were jealous. It's only fair."

"Because you've got Michael to be jealous of."

"Exactly."

"Okay," she said. "You've got a deal."

"Is the paper running the story?"

"Sure. It's a pretty big story."

" 'Criminal Defender Paul Cizek Lost at Sea,' " I said. " 'Presumed Drowned.' "

"Something like that." She sighed. "From what you said, it sounds like there's more of a story there than that."

"Maybe there is."

"Any conflict if I look into it?"

"Not so far. Everything I told you up to Olivia's phone call this afternoon is fair game. But since I'm now officially her lawyer, I won't be able to tell you anything after today."

"Cizek was sleeping with that girl?"

"I wouldn't be surprised."

Alex nodded. "Nothing very unusual about that, I guess."

"Aside from the fact that Paul's about twice her age."

"What about this Thomas Gall?" she said.

I shrugged. "He threatened Paul in court, as you remember. He was there today. Maddy Wilkins said she'd seen him with Paul. I suppose an intrepid reporter might want to look into it."

"I'm only going to be intrepid for another couple of months, you know."

"I keep trying not to think about it."

"We'll work it out."

"Sure."

"My lease is up at the end of August. I told my landlord I'm not renewing it. I've got to start looking for a cheap place in the country. Will you help me?"

"Of course."

"Southern Vermont, maybe. Or Maine or New Hampshire. Massachusetts is just too expensive."

I stared out over the harbor.

Alex's hand touched my leg. "It's not exactly Montana, Brady."

"No," I said. "I'd never see you if you went to Montana."

"Unless you came with me. Then we'd see each other all the time, no matter where we were." She laid her head on my shoulder. "I want you to do what you want to do."

"Easier said than done."

"I just hate to see you stuck."

I thought of Paul Cizek. He'd felt stuck. A lot of men my age got stuck. Some of them stayed stuck all their lives. Some of them managed to get unstuck. And some of them tried to unstick themselves and failed to survive the process.

I spotted Gloria standing back from the crowd at the baggage claim area at the United terminal. I took Alex's hand. "Come on," I said to her.

Gloria saw us coming and smiled. I hugged her and she kissed my cheek.

"Gloria," I said, "this is Alex."

They shook hands. "I've read your stuff in the *Globe,*" Gloria said. "You're very good."

"Thanks," said Alex. "Brady's showed me some of your photographs. I like them a lot."

The two of them smiled at each other, and the next thing I knew they were standing there chattering in soft voices, and I had the uncomfortable feeling that they were comparing notes on my various idiosyncrasies and shortcomings.

I kept looking for Joey, and when he appeared I didn't recognize him for an instant. His hair was longer and his tan was deeper than I'd ever seen. When he'd left for California a year earlier, he was a boy. Now he looked like an adult.

"Hey, Dad," he said. He held out his hand. I shook it. We hesitated, then I gave him a hug. "I was hoping you'd be here," he added.

"It was your mother's idea."

"I tried to call," he said. "Got your machine."

"You didn't leave a message."

"I was calling collect." He smiled. "I was at Billy's. I didn't want to stick him with the cost."

Joey gathered his bags and we found a coffee shop in the terminal. Joey told us about his year at Stanford and his visit with his brother in Idaho, and after ten or fifteen minutes he abruptly turned to Gloria and said, "We gotta get going. I told Debbie I'd be there by midnight."

"You have a date?" I said. "At midnight?"

"I haven't seen her in almost a year, Pop."

You haven't seen me for a year, either, I thought. But I just nodded. "That's a long time."

"Neither of us has been going out," he said. "You know how it is."

"I can imagine," I said.

The four of us walked to the parking garage. We stopped at Gloria's car. I shook hands with Joey. "Let me know when you have a day off," I said. "We'll come down and go fishing or something."

"That'd be great," he said.

Alex exchanged kisses with Joey and Gloria. I gave Gloria a hug. Then I took Alex's hand and we went looking for my car.

"Oh, I like her," said Alex as we prowled the aisles of parked cars. "Gloria?"

"Yes. I can see why you married her."

"Can you see why I divorced her?"

She squeezed my arm. "No. But I'm sure you had your reasons."

"We both did."

When we found my car and got in, Alex leaned toward me, put

her arms around my neck, and kissed my ear. "Are you all right?" she whispered.

"Me? Sure. Why?"

"Joey was pretty itchy to leave."

"I remember how it was."

"Kids grow up," she said.

"Yes," I said. "We all do, eventually."

13

The next morning Alex and I took the fat Sunday *Globe* and mugs of coffee out to the balcony. A few puffy white clouds floated in a clear blue sky. The breeze carved whitecaps on the blue water six stories below. White gulls wheeled in the sunlight. Another beautiful blue-and-white June day.

"You don't want to go lie on a beach or something, do you?" I said to Alex.

She was wearing jogging shorts and one of my big, baggy T-shirts. Her long, smooth legs were stretched out in front of her with her heels up on the railing. "God, no," she said. "All that sand and sweat, all those people with bad bodies in skimpy bathing suits throwing Frisbees and playing rap music on their boom boxes and making out on blankets. Are you kidding?"

"Actually, I was."

"You probably want to go fishing."

"Sure. I'd like to go fishing. But I'm not going to."

"You're thinking about Paul Cizek."

"Yes. And Olivia."

"You could worry about them while you're fishing, couldn't you?"

"I couldn't worry properly. The trout would keep interfering.

On the other hand, the worrying would interfere with the fishing. So I think I'll stick close to the phone."

We sipped coffee and kept swapping sections of the newspaper. After a while, Alex took our mugs in for refills, and when she came back she asked for the real estate section. She poked her glasses onto her nose and began studying it with a felt-tipped pen in her hand.

Precisely at noon, she took the real estate pages inside. I remained on the balcony. I could hear Alex talking on the phone. After a while, I wandered inside. She was seated at the kitchen table with the real estate ads spread out in front of her. She had marked them up with her pen, and she was writing notes on a yellow legal pad. The phone was wedged against her ear. She looked up at me, smiled quickly, then dropped her eyes and resumed her conversation.

I refilled my mug and went back out to the balcony.

She was really going to do it.

That evening, Alex and I drove out of the city to David's Bistro in Acton. It was a quiet, intimate little country place where there were no city noises or city people. We parked out back, and when we got out of the car, Alex started for the door but I held her arm. "Wait," I said. "Sniff the air."

She tipped up her head and snuffled loudly. Then she turned to me. "What?"

"A little trout stream flows not far from here. Nashoba Brook. It was one of the places I used to come to on opening day of the fishing season. A long time ago, when I was a kid. Can't you smell it?"

"I guess I don't know what a trout stream is supposed to smell like."

"It smells a lot like the absence of automobile exhaust and hot pavement and electricity," I said. "It smells of cold wet gravel and sun-warmed rocks and mayfly wings."

She sniffed again. "Okay," she said. "Sure. I got it now." She turned and put her arms around my neck. "I'm learning, huh?"

I kissed her forehead. "We're both learning," I said.

The pretty young hostess led us to our favorite corner table. She brought a bourbon old-fashioned for me and a gin and tonic for Alex. We declined appetizers. Alex went for the duckling and I ordered the pork tenderloin.

We touched glasses. "To mayfly wings," said Alex.

We sipped our drinks and Alex started telling me about her latest conversation with her agent, when she abruptly stopped and lifted her eyes. "Hello," she said.

I half turned. Glen Falconer was standing behind my shoulder. "Sorry to bother you," he said. "I saw you come in. Wanted to say hi."

He held out his hand and I took it. "Hi, Glen," I said.

Alex extended her hand toward him. "I'm Alex Shaw," she said.

He shook her hand. "I know," he said. "And I know you know me, too. You covered my trial."

Alex glanced up at Glen, then looked at me.

I frowned at her and mouthed the word "no," but she pretended not to notice. "Won't you sit with us for a minute?" she said.

"Well, sure," said Glen. "Thanks. Just for a minute." He pulled over a chair from an adjacent table and sat down. He had an empty highball glass in his hand. He craned his neck, caught a waitress's attention, and held up his glass. Then he turned to me. "I never thanked you," he said.

"For what?"

"For getting Paul Cizek for me. He saved my ass. Pardon me, Miss Shaw," he said to Alex.

"Brady talks that way all the time," she said.

"That Cizek," said Glen expansively. "Some lawyer. Did a number on dear old Dad, all right." He chuckled. "Did a number on everybody. Witnesses, jury, judge. Reporters, too." He glanced at Alex. "You know what I mean, Miss?"

Alex did not smile. "Sure. I know what you mean."

"I should have gone to prison," said Glen. "And I didn't. How 'bout that?"

"That makes you a lucky guy, I guess," I said. Glen, I realized, had already had a few drinks. His eyes glittered and his movements seemed slow and studied, as if he had to plan them out before making them.

"Anyhow," he continued, "I quit driving."

"Way to go," I said. "Congratulations."

He either ignored or didn't get my sarcasm. "Thanks. I feel good about it. I've got a bicycle, so I can drink all I want, and if I drive drunk, at least the only person I'll hurt will be myself for a while."

"For a while?" I said.

"Oh, I'll climb back behind the wheel one of these days. You can't keep a good man down, huh? But for now it's the bike. That's how I got here. On my bike."

"You pedaled here from Lincoln?" asked Alex.

"Yes, ma'am. Still living with my daddy, riding my bike around town."

"That's a long bike ride, isn't it?" she said. "All the way from Lincoln?"

"I haven't got anything else to do," he said. "I ride the bike everywhere. It passes the time."

The waitress sidled up to the table and placed a fresh highball in front of Glen. She hesitated, then said to me, "Shall I hold your salads for a few minutes?"

"No," I said. "We're starved."

"Another drink, Mr. Coyne? Miss Shaw?"

Alex shook her head. "We're fine, thanks," I said.

"I'll leave you two alone," said Glen. "I just wanted to say hello."

"Sure," I said. "Take it easy."

Glen picked up his drink and took a swallow. "I liked your editorial, by the way," he said to Alex.

"Editorial?" she said.

"The one you wrote the day after the trial. The one saying I should've been thrown in prison."

"That was unsigned," she said. "It represented the editorial position of the paper."

He nodded and smiled. "Sure. But you wrote it. It's okay. It was good. Maybe they *should* have found me guilty." He looked down at the table. "Sometimes I wish they had."

"You've got to live with it," I said.

"It's hard."

"The booze helps, huh?"

He looked up at me. "I can't quit drinking, Brady. So I quit driving cars. I figure if I kill myself, who cares? My life is ruined anyway."

"I think our salads are coming," I said.

Glen frowned at me. "Huh? Oh. Sorry. I'll get back to my table." He stood up, then reached hastily for his chair, which threatened to topple over. "Nice to see you folks. Sorry to interrupt your dinner. I'll just get back to my table now."

With studied precision, Glen turned his chair around and slid it back into its place at the next table. Then he picked up his highball and held it aloft. "Thank you both again," he said solemnly. "Thank you very much."

Alex and I watched him pick his way carefully across the dining room to a table against the far wall.

"He's eating alone," said Alex.

"Don't even think of it."

"Oh, I wasn't," she said. "Still, it's hard not to feel sorry for him."

"Don't," I said. "He doesn't deserve your sympathy. Did you hear him? *His* life is ruined? Like he didn't ruin the lives of that woman and her family?"

She smiled. "You're a hard man, Brady Coyne."

"He should've gone to prison. Did you hear him? He admits he can't quit drinking, and he's looking forward to climbing back behind the wheel."

"I know," she said. "You're right."

"I didn't hear anything like remorse out of him," I said. "Just self-pity. Anyway, he's drinking. He's all set. And one of these days he'll get into a car and smash into somebody else."

Our waitress brought our salads and ground some black pepper onto them. "Anything else, folks?"

"Let's have some wine," said Alex.

"Not me," I said.

"*We* are not drunks," she said.

I looked at her. "You're right. I'm sorry." I glanced at the card on the table listing David's recommended wines. "The sauvignon blanc?"

"Yes," said Alex.

After our waitress left, I reached for Alex's hand. "Did I misbehave?"

"No. You were rude to Glen, but he deserved it."

"I didn't embarrass you?"

"You never embarrass me."

"I embarrass myself sometimes."

"That's another thing I love about you," she said. "You're such a sensitive guy."

"Oh, shit," I mumbled. "Anything but that."

We ate our salads in silence, and then Alex patted her mouth with her napkin and said, "Brady?"

"Um?"

"We've got to talk about what we're going to do."

"What I'm going to do when you move, you mean."

She nodded. "Yes."

"Now?"

She cocked her head and smiled. "No. Not now. Let's just have a nice meal. Now I want you to tell me all about what it was like when you were a little boy on opening day of the fishing season."

"It always rained," I said.

A string quartet was playing on the PBS radio station as we drove back to the city, and we listened to it without talking. After a while, Alex murmured, "Brady?"

"Hm?"

"I don't mean to pressure you."

"You aren't, are you?"

"Not intentionally. Do you feel pressured?"

"Sometimes a man needs a nudge," I said.

"There's plenty of time," she said. "Just try to figure out what you really want."

"Easier said than done." After a minute, I said, "You know what I really want?"

She reached over and squeezed my leg. I heard her chuckle. "Yes," she said. "I think so."

14

I beat Julie to the office on Monday and had the coffee all brewed for her. We sat in my office while I recounted the events of the weekend—my late-night phone call from Olivia Cizek, the people I had talked to in Newburyport, my Thomas Gall sighting, my encounter with the drunken Glen Falconer.

When I told her that Alex and I had met Joey's plane, and that Gloria had been there, Julie's eyebrows went up. "How did it go?"

"Go?"

"You know. How'd Gloria react?"

"It was Gloria's idea," I said. "She reacted fine. They both did. Everybody did."

"Sometimes," said Julie, "I don't get it."

"Gloria and I have been divorced for a long time," I said gently.

She was shaking her head. "I know. Still . . ."

"Things change. You move on."

"I always thought—"

"That Gloria and I would get back together. I know. I used to think that sometimes. But we're not going to."

"You love Alex."

"Yes. I like Gloria. I care about her. I think she likes me, too.

We've become friends. But I love Alex, and I think Gloria approves."

Julie reached across my desk and put her hand on my cheek. "I do, too," she said. "You've been happy with Alex."

I thought of Alex moving to Vermont or Maine, and I wondered if I'd still be happy then. I decided not to discuss it with Julie. Not yet. I had to decide what I was going to do first.

I cleared my throat. "Not to change the subject," I said, "but I think we better get to work. First off, let's draw up a standard retainer contract for Olivia Cizek."

"That poor woman," said Julie.

I nodded.

"She must be feeling terribly guilty."

"Guilty?"

"The marriage failed. He left her. And now . . . "

"If she'd been a better wife it never would've happened," I said. "Is that what you mean?"

"It's what she'd think."

"It's not as if she abandoned him," I said. "It was the other way around. Why should she feel guilty?"

"It's how women are, Brady."

"Oh."

"Mr. and Mrs. Cizek already have an agreement with us, you know," she said. "Do you think a separate one with her is necessary?"

"Not really. But it's what she wants."

"Okay. Can do." Julie stood up and smoothed her skirt against the sides of her legs. "Check your In box, Brady." She started for the door, then turned. "I'm glad Gloria is okay," she said.

"She is," I said. "I promise."

Julie went out to her desk and I sat behind mine. My In box, as usual, was piled with papers that needed pushing.

So I pushed them around for a while. My mind kept wandering to Olivia and Paul. I called Olivia at home. Her machine invited me to leave a message. "It's Brady," I told it. "Monday morning. I'll try your office."

Olivia was unable to come to the phone, her secretary told me.

I left my name and number, emphasized that it was not urgent, and asked to have her return my call.

Then I called the Newburyport police. Lieutenant Kirschenbaum was on another line. I agreed to hold. I waited for the length of time it took me to smoke a cigarette before he growled, "Kirschenbaum."

"It's Brady Coyne, Lieutenant," I said. "I'm—"

"I remember you," he said. "The Cizek thing. What's up?"

"I wondered if you had any news."

"No."

"They haven't found Paul's body, then."

"I guess that would qualify as news, Mr. Coyne, don't you think?"

"I guess it would."

"That's why you called?"

"No," I said. "I wanted to share something with you."

"Sharing is good. One of those virtues you learn in kindergarten. Some guy made millions on a book about all the good stuff you learn in kindergarten. Share away, Mr. Coyne."

I told him about my conversation with Dolph at the boat ramp, my examination of Paul's boat at the Coast Guard station, and my visit with Maddy Wilkins at Paul's cottage on Plum Island. "And when I left," I said, "Thomas Gall was standing there outside the house. When I called to him, he walked away, got in his truck, and drove off. You know who Thomas Gall is, don't you?"

"Refresh my memory."

"This past winter Paul Cizek defended the man who killed Gall's wife in an auto accident. The jury came back with a 'not guilty' verdict. At the end of the trial, Gall threatened Paul. He yelled, 'I'll get you,' or something to that effect."

"So you think he got him, huh?"

"I don't know what to think. The girl said he'd been there before. So he knew where Paul was staying. If anybody had a motive—"

"We don't even know if Cizek's dead, Mr. Coyne. All we know is that his boat was adrift in the storm."

"He wasn't fishing. There was no bait aboard. So why was he out there?" I paused, then said, "According to his wife, he was not heavily insured, by the way."

Kirschenbaum chuckled. "Yeah, I thought of that."

"I thought you might have. I suppose you could check on the insurance, but—"

"Look," said Kirschenbaum, "I appreciate your help, I really do. I'll keep this Gall in mind. But, you know, we law enforcement people pretty much limit our work to solving crimes and apprehending criminals, and so far we don't seem to have a crime here. All we've got is a boat, you know?"

"Sure. I know that."

"But you're trying to make a murder case out of this."

"No, I'm not. I'd rather Paul was alive. But it doesn't look like he is."

I heard Kirschenbaum sigh. "No, it doesn't look that way, and I really don't mean to be short with you. I'm glad you told me about this Gall character and the insurance thing. Anything else, don't hesitate to call. Okay?"

"Okay."

"And if we learn anything, I'll pass it along to Mrs. Cizek."

"Since I'm her lawyer," I said, "it might be better if you pass it along to me."

"Because if it's bad news, you should be the one to break it to her. You being more sensitive and caring than me."

"Exactly," I said.

Olivia returned my call around noontime. "Have you heard something?" she said.

"No. Nothing. You?"

I heard her sigh. "No."

"I'm glad you're working," I said.

"It gives me something to do." She hesitated. "Brady?"

"Yes?"

"I think it would be better if you didn't call unless you had something to tell me. I mean, I appreciate your concern, but when

I saw that message from you, my heart started pounding and I felt like I had to throw up. Right now I'm figuring that no news is— well, at least no news is not bad news. I was so grateful to be able to come to work today. The weekend was hard. This gives me other things to think about. Do you understand?"

"Sure," I said. "No problem. I do understand."

"You're awfully sweet. And I do want to put this on a businesslike basis."

"I'm having Julie draw up a contract. We'll send it out to you this afternoon. And we'll do business when and if there's business to be done."

"Good," she said. "I'll sign it and write you a check and get it back to you."

"It's not necessary, you know."

"I'm more comfortable with it this way."

I ushered the day's last client out of my office on Wednesday afternoon. It was four o'clock, which, if I didn't dillydally, would give me just enough time to zip home, change my clothes, gather up some gear, and drive out to the Squannacook River in Townsend, where the trout would be feeding on mayflies. An attractive plan, I thought. I would do it. I owed myself one.

About then Julie tapped on the door, pushed it open, and stuck her head into my office. Her eyebrows were arched in her "May I come in?" expression. I crooked my finger at her, and she came in.

She closed the door behind her and stood in front of my desk. "Brady," she said, "there's a man here who wants to see you."

"He doesn't have an appointment?"

"No."

"You never let anyone see me without an appointment," I said. "I was actually thinking of going fishing."

"He's been waiting all afternoon. I told him you'd see him when you were done."

I slumped back in my chair. "He must be awfully persuasive. Or desperate. What's he want?"

"I don't know. He's desperate, I think. He came in, said he

needed to see you, and when I told him he could make an appointment, he just sat down and said he'd wait. I told him you were tied up all afternoon, and he said that was okay. He's been sitting there jiggling his knee and flipping through your old *Field & Streams*."

"You're telling me I should see him."

She nodded.

"Even though he doesn't have an appointment and he's not one of our clients."

She shrugged.

"The whole damn trout season is passing me by."

"He seems like a nice, quiet man with big problems."

"Fine. Okay. I'll see him." I shook my finger at her. "But don't you ever again accuse me of being a softie when I make house calls or forget to record all my billable time," I said, in what I thought was a convincing growl.

Julie grinned, came around the desk, and planted a wet kiss on my cheek. "You're a nice man," she said.

"I'm a sucker, is what I am," I said.

She went out, and a minute later she came back, followed by a short, round man with a high forehead and gray hair and dark eyes. He wore khaki pants and a green linen sport jacket, blue-and-white striped shirt, no tie, and a shy smile.

"Mr. Coyne," said Julie, "this is Mr. Vaccaro."

I stared at the man for a moment, then nodded. The last time I'd seen him, he'd been wearing a camel-hair topcoat in Skeeter's Infield, and he'd been talking to Paul Cizek. "We've met," I said to Julie. "Thanks."

She frowned for an instant, then shrugged and left the office, closing the door behind her.

I settled back in my chair. "What can I do for you, Mr. Vaccaro?"

"I need a lawyer."

"Who referred you to me?"

"No one. At least, not exactly. See, Mr. Cizek is my regular lawyer. Paul Cizek?"

I nodded. "Go ahead."

"Well, Mr. Cizek defended me. Almost two years ago, it was. And now—"

"I know all about you," I said.

He looked at me without expression.

"You work for the Russo family," I said. "Vinny Russo pays you to kill people. You shoot them in the eye. You're famous for that. You murdered an old man in a North End restaurant."

He shrugged. "They found me innocent."

"They found you not guilty," I said, "which is a lot different. Look, Mr. Vaccaro. I don't know what your problem is, but I'm not a criminal lawyer. I can't help you."

"You mean you don't want to help me," he said.

I nodded. "Yes, that's right."

"Mr. Cizek is missing," he said. "I need him."

I didn't say anything.

Vaccaro leaned forward. "You're looking for him. So am I. We can help each other."

"What makes you think I'm looking for him?"

He sat back in his chair and shrugged.

I lit a cigarette and looked at him through the smoke. "Why did you come here, Mr. Vaccaro?"

"I want Mr. Cizek. Look, can I tell you about it?"

I shrugged. "You've already ruined my fishing plans. Go ahead."

"Okay." He took a deep breath. "Okay," he said again. "Yeah, the cops had me by the nuts for poppin' that old guy in Natalie's. What they wanted was for me to give them Vinny Russo. You know, testify against him. They knew I coulda done it. I give them Uncle Vinny, they let me go. You know, move me someplace, give me a new name and some money. I told 'em no fuckin' way. I know how those deals work. The Russos'd find me in a month. I'd be a dead man. I told 'em to go fuck themselves. I'm better off going on trial. I figured they'd put me away. But Uncle Vinny got Mr. Cizek to defend me and he got me off."

"So what's your problem?"

He narrowed his eyes. "Now I think that prick Russo's gonna have me hit. I stood up for the son of a bitch, and now he decides he don't trust me. I wanna go back to the feds and give 'em Vinny and every other fuckin' Russo in Boston."

"Good idea," I said. "Do it. It's your civic responsibility."

He didn't smile. "It ain't that easy, Mr. Coyne."

"I don't want to hear this," I said. "You should go find yourself a lawyer who can help you."

"There's only one lawyer I trust. I gotta have Mr. Cizek. So you gotta find him for me. You find him and tell him I need him."

"As far as I know," I said, "Paul Cizek went overboard Friday night. They haven't found his body, but—"

"He's alive," said Vaccaro.

"What makes you think so?"

He shrugged. "He's gotta be alive. I need him."

"Well, I tell you what," I said. "If I see him, I'll give him your message. How's that?"

"Don't fuck with me, Mr. Coyne," he said softly. "I give you respect. You shouldn't disrespect me."

"Frankly, Mr. Vaccaro," I said, "I don't see any reason why I should respect you, and I don't think there's anything left for us to discuss."

"You kicking me out?" he said.

"I think you said what you had to say. Your appointment is over."

He stared at me for a moment, then shrugged. He reached into his jacket pocket and withdrew a roll of bills. He removed several of them one at a time and made a stack on my desk.

I pushed it away. "I don't want your money."

"You better take it."

"I'm not your lawyer. I don't want you for a client."

"You don't get it," he said. "You gotta be my lawyer."

"No, I don't. My clients are all people who I want to help. People I like and care about. I'm the one who decides who my clients are."

He smiled. "Yeah, that's pretty good, Mr. Coyne. I like that." His smile abruptly vanished. He leaned forward and peered at me with his hard little black eyes. "I know how it works, and so do you. I told you all this. I told you I was ready to give Uncle Vinny to the feds. That's important information. If it got out, it'd be bad for me. I can't have that happen. If you're my lawyer, you can't tell anyone else. If you're my lawyer, I can trust you. So you better take the money, Mr. Coyne, see?"

"Are you threatening me, Mr. Vaccaro?" I said quietly.

He waved his hand. "I'm just trying to hire a lawyer."

"And if I refuse to be hired?"

He leaned back, spread his hands, and smiled. "Please," he said. "Take the money."

I picked up the stack of bills from my desk. I counted them. There were twenty fifties. I took three of them and pushed the rest away. "Okay," I said. "That covers the time you've been here. So you can trust me. Now your appointment is over."

"Now you can't tell anybody what I told you."

"That's right."

He pushed the money back toward me. "Take more than that," he said.

"This is my regular fee."

"Go ahead. I've got plenty of money."

"So do I," I said.

He shrugged, picked up the stack of bills, and shoved it into his jacket pocket. "You tell Mr. Cizek I need him."

"I don't expect to see Paul Cizek."

"But if you do?"

"I'll tell him," I said.

"Good," he said. He stood up and held out his hand to me.

I did not shake it.

15

Julie stared at me. "He's a *what*?"

"A hit man," I said. "A murderer. An assassin for hire."

"But he seemed—"

"Like a nice, quiet man."

"Well, he did."

"Desperate, I think you said."

Julie nodded.

"He's desperate, all right. And quiet. But he's not nice."

She dropped into the armchair in my office and began hugging herself and shaking her head. "You mean he really—"

"Eddie Vaccaro makes his living by shooting people he doesn't even know," I said. "He does it without emotion. It's his profession. He uses a twenty-two automatic pistol. He usually puts the first one in their eye and another behind their ear."

"And I made you see him," she said.

I shrugged. "It's okay. I won't see him again."

"I'm sorry, Brady."

I patted her arm. "Don't worry about it." I decided not to tell her that *I* was worried about it. I didn't like having killers share their life-and-death secrets with me.

"So what did he want?" she said.

"He wants Paul Cizek. He said he's in trouble and needs a lawyer. Apparently Paul is the only one he trusts."

"Why come to you?"

"I don't know," I said. "He thinks I'm looking for Paul."

"Why would he think that?"

"I don't know," I said. "I don't even know if Vaccaro was telling me the truth."

Julie frowned. "If he was lying—"

"Let's not think about it," I said quickly. "It's time to go home."

Of course, I did think about it. I thought about it while I walked home from the office, and I thought about it while I sat on my balcony sipping Rebel Yell on the rocks, and I thought about it while I stared up into the darkness with Alex sleeping beside me that night.

If Vaccaro had been lying about the reason he wanted to find Paul Cizek, it meant he wanted him for something else.

If he'd been lying about the fact that he didn't know where Paul was, it meant he *did* know what had happened to him.

I decided I might as well assume Vaccaro had been telling me the truth. I figured being lied to by a Mafia hit man was bad news by definition.

And if Eddie Vaccaro had been telling me the truth, of course, it meant that he hadn't killed Paul.

And I fell asleep hoping that I'd done the right thing, accepting his money. I don't think I'd have fallen asleep at all if I had refused it. Anybody who killed people for money wouldn't hesitate to kill them for their silence.

Olivia called shortly after I arrived at the office on Friday morning. "I wonder if you can give me a hand," she said.

"I'll try," I said. "What's up?"

"The Coast Guard called. They want Paul's boat moved. I told them I'd arrange to come get it."

"When?"

"It's got to be this weekend. They said they'd have to dispose of it if it wasn't gone by Sunday."

"Can you get off this afternoon?"

"Let me check." A moment later she said, "I could meet you at that Friendly's ice cream place at four. Can you do that?"

"That'll work," I said. "We'll have to get Paul's car, because we need the trailer. Do you have a key?"

"To his car? No, I don't."

"There's probably a spare one at his cottage. We'll have to check there." I thought we could look around, and if we didn't find Paul's spare ignition key, Maddy Wilkins might help. I decided not to mention Maddy to Olivia unless it was necessary. "Okay," I said. "Friendly's at four. I'll be there."

"Brady," said Olivia, "you haven't heard anything, have you?"

I thought of my visit from Eddie Vaccaro. "No. We agreed not to keep calling each other unless we knew something. I've heard nothing."

"Me neither," she said.

Olivia was leaning against her red Saab with her face tilted up to the sun when I pulled into the lot at Friendly's. She was wearing sneakers and tight-fitting jeans and a plaid cotton shirt with the sleeves rolled up to her elbows, and she was sipping through a straw from a Friendly's cardboard drinking container, and for an instant I could picture her as a young, carefree college kid with nothing better to do than sip a soda and enjoy the sunshine. When she saw me, she waved, came over, and climbed in beside me.

"Another beautiful June afternoon," I said lamely.

"Yes, it is," she said. "Perfect."

I pulled out of the lot and headed into Newburyport. "How have you been?"

She laughed quickly. "I guess I've been numb. I have these—these moments. When it hits me. It's worst at night, when I'm home alone. I've been watching a lot of television. But mostly I just live my life. It's been a week. It seems like forever since I got that call. It was a week ago tonight."

I drove down High Street, onto Water Street, and out past the Coast Guard station, heading for Plum Island.

"How are we going to get into his place?" said Olivia.

"I know where the key's hidden."

She didn't ask how I knew, so I didn't have to mention Maddy.

And since Maddy's old yellow Volkswagen was not parked in Paul's yard when we got there, I still didn't have to mention her to Olivia. The newly planted petunias looked pink and perky in their little flower bed in the front yard. The key was still under the flower pot on the deck, and I used it to let us in.

Olivia looked around and smiled. "He wasn't much for picking up after himself," she said, and I didn't miss her use of the past tense. I figured that somewhere in her unconscious she'd already accepted the likelihood that Paul was dead.

There was a kitchen/dining room/living room area with a single picture window that overlooked the marsh. Beyond the living room were two closed doors—bedrooms, I assumed—and one open one, a bathroom. The decor was neo–K Mart—spindly chairs, a round pine table, matching pseudo-colonial sofa and armchair. Magazines and newspapers and shoes and socks littered the floor and furniture. Unopened mail was scattered across the top of the table. The kitchen sink was piled with pots and dishes.

"Where do we start?" said Olivia.

I shrugged. "We're all creatures of habit. Where did Paul usually keep his spare keys?"

"In his desk drawer." She looked around. "I don't see a desk in this place."

"There's probably a chest of drawers in his bedroom. Or maybe the spare bedroom has a desk in it." I gestured toward the closed doors. "Why don't you look around in there. I'll check out here."

Olivia headed for the bedrooms. I rummaged through the two drawers that bracketed the sink. One held a jumble of forks and knives and spoons and spatulas and can openers. There were screwdrivers and pliers and a hammer and an assortment of other junk in the other one. No keys. Nothing on the windowsill or on top of the refrigerator.

I sat at the kitchen table. A bunch of limp daisies drooped in a water glass. From Maddy, I guessed. I picked up a stack of mail and glanced through it. Mostly junk stuff addressed to "Occupant." I figured Paul hadn't gotten around to having his address permanently changed.

There were a few bills—electricity, water, telephone—a bank statement, some catalogs, a couple of *Newsweek* magazines.

No mysterious letters. Nothing to indicate what might've happened to him.

From one of the bedrooms, Olivia called, "Got it." She came out holding up a key. "This has to be it," she said.

"Good," I said. "Let's go do it."

She stood in the living room and nudged a balled-up sweatshirt with her toe. "This is spooky," she said.

"Being here?"

She nodded. "I mean, I *know* these clothes." She waved her hand at the shoes and T-shirts and socks scattered on the floor. "I've picked them up a hundred times. I've picked up his pants and shirts, washed them, folded them, hung them up . . . "

I went to her and touched her arm. "Olivia."

She looked up at me and smiled quickly. "I'm okay, Brady." She took a long look around the inside of the cottage, shook her head, and went outside.

We drove to the boat ramp. Paul's car was still parked there, and the key opened the door and fit into the ignition. Olivia got in and followed me to the Coast Guard station. We drove directly down to the dock, and by the time we had climbed out of the cars, a young guy had hurried down to join us.

"Something I can help you with, sir?" he said to me.

"We came to get the Whaler," I said, pointing at Paul's boat.

"Why don't you just hang on for a second." He turned and jogged back to the brick building, and a few minutes later the officer whom I'd seen on my previous visit strode down to us.

"Mr. Coyne," he said. "You've come for the boat."

I nodded. "This is Mrs. Cizek. The Whaler belongs to her husband."

He nodded to her and mumbled, "Ma'am." He turned to me. "No news, huh?"

I shook my head.

"Well, the Newburyport police tell us they're done with the boat, and we don't have any space for it, so I'm glad you can take it."

"Want me to back down?" said Olivia.

I laughed. "I'd be relieved. I'm not very good at backing trailers down boat ramps. I tend to bump into things."

"I've done it plenty of times," she said, and she proceeded to do it expertly.

A half hour later we had parked boat, trailer, and car in the side yard of Paul's cottage. Olivia insisted on returning the car key to where she had found it. Then we drove back to the Friendly's lot in my car.

Olivia suggested we have coffee, but I declined. It was Alex's turn to cook dinner, and I didn't want to be late, even if it turned out to be lentil soup.

16

Alex was out on the balcony when I got home. She was wearing a pair of my boxer shorts and her own "Walk for Hunger" T-shirt. She was tilted back in one of the aluminum chairs with her legs up on the railing and her eyes closed.

I eased up her T-shirt to expose some smooth skin and kissed her belly. Her fingers moved in my hair. "Mmm," she said. "Nice. What was that for?"

"Does it have to be *for* something?"

"It's better if it isn't," she said.

"It's because I don't smell lentil soup."

She grabbed a handful of my hair, pulled my head up, and clamped both arms around my neck. She put her mouth on my ear and whispered, "Hungry?"

"How do you mean that?"

She kissed my mouth, then sat up. "For now, I'm talking about dinner. Go grab yourself a beer and then stay out of my kitchen. I'll call you to the table."

"You're awfully sexy when you're bossy," I said. "And you're particularly sexy in my boxer shorts." I snapped her a salute. "I will obey, sir."

I changed into my jeans and took a beer onto the balcony, where

I watched the setting sun splash colors on the cloud bank that was building on the horizon. Thoughts of Eddie Vaccaro and Paul Cizek flitted in and out of my consciousness. I willed myself not to focus on them, and had good success at it.

An hour or so later Alex called, "Come and get it." I went to the table.

Grilled lamb chops, boiled potatoes doused with melted butter and sprinkled with parsley, stir-fried snow peas, avocado on beds of Bibb lettuce, a sweet German wine. "You're an amazing woman," I said to Alex. "Do you make your own clothes, too?"

"No, I steal them from men," she said. "Tomorrow's Saturday. Are you going fishing tomorrow?"

"I'd like to. I'm going to call Charlie."

I did, and he was eager. We debated our options and decided on the Farmington River in Connecticut. We always found rising trout on the Farmington. I told him I'd pick him up at eight.

At six in the morning, when I woke up, an easterly wind was driving hard raindrops against the windows. They sounded like buckshot rattling on the glass. I stood there sipping my coffee and staring down through the sliding doors at the gray, churning surface of the harbor.

I felt Alex's hand on the back of my neck. Then her arms went around my chest and I felt her breasts pressing against my back. "It's a pretty lousy day," she murmured.

"Too lousy for trout fishing."

"I thought rain was good for fishing."

"No. That's a fallacy. This kind of rain ruins trout fishing. The Farmington will be high and muddy and the trout will be sulking on the bottom. Besides, it's no fun getting soaked."

"Macho-type men like confronting the elements, don't they? Isn't getting wet and freezing your ass off what it's all about?"

"No. Enjoying a pleasant June day and catching trout on dry flies is what it's all about."

"I'm sorry," she said. "I guess you'll go tomorrow, huh?"

"No," I said. "Tomorrow is Sunday, our only day together. Charlie and I can go fishing next Saturday."

"You can go tomorrow, Brady. I understand."

I turned around and hugged her. "It's not a sacrifice, you know, spending a day with you."

She looked up at me. "Mean it?"

I kissed her. "Yes."

She took my hand. "Since it's raining and you can't go fishing," she said, "you might as well come back to bed."

"I already had a mug of coffee. I'll never get back to sleep."

"Exactly," she said.

Sunday, of course, dawned clear and sunny. It would've been a perfect day for trout fishing.

"Why don't you go?" said Alex as we spread marmalade on English muffins at the table.

"I want to be with you."

"You deserve a nice fishing trip."

"One of these days, maybe I'll have one," I said. "Anyway, I also deserve a nice day with you."

"Well," she said, "we're going for a drive. You can bring your stuff, maybe stop somewhere along the way."

"Where are we going?"

"Maine."

"Is this a real estate excursion?"

She nodded.

"I thought you were interested in Vermont."

"I was. I've made a lot of calls. Vermont's too expensive. There are places in Maine I can afford. I found a nice real estate lady who's got several places for me to look at."

"How far up?"

"Not far. Maybe three hours from here."

"I don't know any good trout rivers in southern Maine."

She reached across the table and touched my hand. "Brady, I mean it," she said. "I wish you'd go fishing."

"I mean it, too," I said. "I want to go to Maine with you. I want to help you find a nice place to live."

★　★　★

Alex hugged my arm. "Oh, Brady," she said. "This is it. Don't you think?"

It was just the third place we'd looked at, a modest post-and-beam home that sat on a dirt road in Garrison, Maine, due west of Portland near the New Hampshire border. The entire first floor was a single open room with a wooden spiral staircase leading to the upstairs. A big picture window overlooked a valley and low rolling hills beyond. There was a wood stove at one end and a big fieldstone fireplace at the other. A fairly modern kitchen extended across half of the back wall. The double windows over the sink looked out into the woods.

Upstairs there were three decent-sized bedrooms and a bath. The place hadn't been lived in for a year, and the monthly rent had been reduced a few times. Now it was half what Alex was paying for her two-bedroom apartment on Marlborough Street in Boston.

The real estate agent, a gray-haired woman named Alice, said that the town kept the dirt road plowed in the winter, and a local man would keep her supplied with firewood and perform a variety of handyman chores.

"I think it's perfect," I said to Alex.

"But—"

"But nothing. It's perfect. Grab it."

She did. We drove back to the real estate office, where Alex signed a one-year renewable lease and wrote a check for two months' rent. The place would be hers on the first of September.

I bought us each a Pepsi at a Maine backroad mom-and-pop store on the way home. We leaned against the side of the car outside the store. I held up my Pepsi can. "To your new home," I said.

She gave me a small smile, then touched her can to mine.

"You're thinking it could be *our* new home?" I said.

She shrugged. "Something like that. Yes."

I nodded. "I guess it could. It's a nice place. I like it."

"I will never pressure you," she said. "You see the place. You know what it is. You know I'm going to be living there. Now you've got to decide what to do."

"Yes, I do. I don't have a choice. If I don't decide, that will be a decision, too."

"I'll love you no matter what you do," she said.

Yes, I thought. But it would never be quite the same.

We didn't talk much on the way home. I wanted to be more enthusiastic for Alex. I just couldn't fake it. And I suspected she was struggling to dampen her own enthusiasm out of deference to my feelings.

We stopped at a little Italian restaurant in Burlington for supper. The pasta was good and we split a carafe of the house wine. Alex chatted about her book and a couple of stories she was working on, trying very hard to avoid the subject we were both thinking about. I nodded and smiled in the right places, but after a while our conversation petered out.

It was dark when we got back to the city. I pulled into my parking slot beside Alex's car. "I think I'll go home now," said Alex.

"Oh?"

She tried to give me a bright smile. "I've got a busy day tomorrow."

"Sure. And you probably have laundry to do. Wash your hair, pay your bills, make some phone calls—"

She grabbed my arm. "Listen to me."

"I'm sorry," I said. "I was being childish."

"So was I," she said. "I wasn't saying what I meant. Let me try again."

I touched her face. "Okay."

"I just think . . . if I stayed tonight we'd feel—tension. I really don't want to influence your thinking. I'm not sure I know how to act right now. I'm excited by my new place. I'm sad because it's making a problem for you. Do you see?"

"I think so." I smiled. "Is this our first fight?" I tried to make it come out like a joke, but it didn't sound like one, even to my ears.

Alex shrugged. "We're—having a conflict. I'm sorry. I don't want to fight or argue or do anything but be happy with you. I don't want to be apart from you, but I'm going to be living in Maine, for the next two years. I really want to share my life with you. I want you to want that, too."

"It's not that I don't want to share my life with you," I said.

She looked at me for a moment, then nodded. "I believe you."

"You won't stay with me tonight?"

She shook her head. "No. I don't think I should. Not tonight. It'll be easier for you if I'm not around."

"Maybe you're right," I said.

She put her arms around my neck and gave me a long, hungry kiss. When she pulled back, her eyes were glistening.

When I got up to my apartment, I sloshed some Rebel Yell into a glass, added three ice cubes, and went out on the balcony. I sat there in the dark for a long time, sipping my drink and smoking cigarettes and watching the play of lights over the harbor.

After awhile I went to bed.

My pillow smelled like Alex's hair. I stared up at the ceiling. It took a while, but eventually I fell asleep.

The next morning I noticed that the light on my answering machine was blinking. I had forgotten to check it when I got home after my day of house-hunting with Alex.

I pressed the button. The machine whirred. Then a voice said, "Mr. Coyne, this is Brenda Falconer. Glen's wife. It's Sunday, around three in the afternoon. Something has happened. The Senator wants you to call him at home."

17

I poured a mug of coffee, lit a cigarette, and dialed Roger Falconer's number in Lincoln. After several rings, a woman's voice said, "Yes?"

"May I speak with Roger?"

"Who's calling?"

"It's Brady Coyne. Is this Brenda?"

"Yes. I'm sorry. I was sleeping. I had a late night." She paused, and I heard rustling noises that suggested she was sitting up in bed. "Thanks for calling back. The Senator's not here. I know he's eager to talk to you."

"Your message said something had happened."

"Oh, geez. You don't know."

"Know what?"

"Glen's in the hospital."

"What happened?"

"We're not sure. It was a bicycle accident. He's—he's in bad shape."

"How bad?"

"He's been unconscious since they found him. That was Sunday morning. He's got a fractured skull, broken pelvis, internal injuries."

"He was on his bike?"

I heard a short, ironic laugh. "Yes. He was apparently driving drunk again, only this time he didn't kill anybody except maybe himself. Since his last, um, accident, he's stopped driving automobiles. He's too weak to quit drinking, so he quit driving. He pedals around the back roads of Lincoln and Concord and Sudbury to the houses of people who will give him booze, and to bars and restaurants, and he gets plastered and brags about staying out of prison and talks about driving automobiles again pretty soon, and then he wobbles home. Saturday night he didn't make it. Some joggers found him in the morning, lying in the weeds beside the road near the river at Nine Acre Corner. They figure he'd been there for several hours, bleeding and his brain swelling." She blew out a breath. "I'm sorry to rattle on like this. It's been pretty stressful around here lately."

"Where is he?" I said.

"Emerson Hospital. His father spent the night there. He'd like to see you."

"Why does he want to see me?"

"I don't know, Mr. Coyne. I think he just needs comforting, and there's nobody else to give it to him."

I inferred that either Roger's daughter-in-law lacked the inclination to offer him comfort, or he lacked the inclination to accept it from her. "Okay," I said. "I'll be there in an hour."

I called the office and left a message on the machine, telling Julie that something had come up and I'd probably not get in much before noontime. Then I showered, got dressed, and took a mug of coffee down to my car.

I pulled into the visitors' lot at Emerson Hospital in Concord a little after eight. The woman at the desk said Glen Falconer was in the intensive care unit and told me how to find it.

Roger was sprawled on a chair in the waiting room. His legs were stretched out in front of him and his arms were folded across his chest and his head was thrown back. He was wearing a wrinkled seersucker suit. His necktie was pulled loose around his neck, and he looked more like someone who'd just crawled in from a bench on the Common than a man people called "Senator" out of respect for his power and wealth. His mouth was open and his eyes were closed and white whiskers sprouted on his jaw, and for the first time in my memory he looked older than his years rather than younger.

I sat in the chair beside him and poked his arm. "Hey, Roger," I said in a loud whisper.

He mumbled something, took a quick breath, and sat up. "What?" He looked at me. "Oh. Brady. What happened? What time is it?"

"You want some coffee or something?"

"Huh? Oh. No. Did you hear anything?"

"I just got here. Brenda called. It's Monday morning, around eight."

"I must've gone to sleep. They don't tell you anything around here."

"I'm sure if there was any news, they'd tell you."

"He didn't die, I guess."

"I think we should get some coffee and breakfast. What do you say?"

"I should be here."

"I'll tell them we'll be in the cafeteria. If there's any news, they'll find us. How's that?"

He shrugged. "Sure. Okay."

So I found a nurse and told her where we'd be, and then I took Roger's arm and steered him down the elevator to the cafeteria. I sat him at a table and then got coffee, juice, and muffins for both of us.

"I've been here since yesterday morning," he told me as he spread butter on his muffin. "They treat me like . . . " He shook his head.

"They probably treat you the same way they treat everybody else," I said. "Their job is to take care of the sick people."

He looked up at me and nodded. "He's going to have brain damage, even if he lives. He may stay unconscious for a long time. Maybe forever. They'll try to keep him alive with machines. They think his kidneys might be lacerated or something."

126

I touched his arm. "I'm sorry."

He picked up his muffin, looked at it, and then put it down. "I've been thinking about it," he said. "I think he wanted this to happen. I think that's why he kept getting drunk and riding his bike around at night. He wanted something to happen to him, the way something happened to that woman he hit." He sighed. "My son isn't much, I know. He's never accomplished anything, and he's a drunk. But, as your friend Cizek was so quick to tell everybody who'd listen, it wasn't Glen's fault."

"It wasn't?"

"No. It was mine."

"I bumped into Glen at a restaurant last week," I said. "He didn't seem particularly remorseful."

Roger nodded. "It's hard to be objective about one's own son. But I love him."

"What *did* happen, do they know?"

Roger shook his head. "I haven't talked to anybody. The police called and said he was here, so I came over, and I've been here ever since. The only people I've talked to have been doctors and nurses. The best they've been able to tell me is that he hasn't died yet."

We finished our skimpy breakfasts, and Roger wanted to go back to the ICU. I convinced him we'd do just as well waiting in the cafeteria for awhile, so I went back and joined the line to get us more coffee.

When I returned to the table, a black-haired fortyish man in a business suit was sitting with Roger. They both looked up at me, as if I'd interrupted something. I slid Roger's cup of coffee in front of him, then sat down.

"This is Brady Coyne," said Roger to the other guy. "He's my attorney."

"Dick Carlson," said the man, extending his hand. "Concord police."

"Lieutenant Carlson's a detective," said Roger.

I shook Carlson's hand.

"Start over," said Roger to Carlson. "I want Brady to hear it."

Carlson nodded, then turned to me. He had sharp gray eyes and a mouth that seemed too small for his face. "Basically," he said, "it looks like a hit and run. We think a car traveling at a high rate of speed ran into him head-on and kept going. There's no other way to explain it. The, um, the extent of the injuries. The bike is completely mangled. Somebody on a bike'd have to be going about sixty and run into a brick wall for that kind of thing to happen."

"Head-on?" I said.

Carlson nodded. "Looks that way."

"He couldn't have just run into a tree or something?" said Roger.

Carlson shook his head. "There wasn't any tree. Just thick weeds. Oh, he'd have hurt himself if he took a tumble. Maybe broken an arm or something. But not a fractured skull."

"So what are you thinking?" I said.

He shrugged. "Kids out late driving too fast, maybe they've had too many beers, they come around the corner and there's this guy riding a bike, weaving down the middle of the road. They hit him, he goes flying, they panic and keep going." He shrugged again.

"Any way to verify that?"

"The state police lab has the bike. Maybe they'll find traces of automobile paint or something on it."

"What can we do?" said Roger.

"I don't know, sir," said Carlson. "Pray for your son, I guess. I just wanted you to know what was going on. We'll find 'em sooner or later. There'll be dents and scrapes on their car. If it was kids, their old man'll see it or someone's conscience will get to them. You can't keep something like that quiet for very long." He glanced at his wristwatch, then stood up. "I've gotta go. I'll keep in touch with you."

He shook hands with Roger, then with me, and started for the door.

"I'll be right back," I said to Roger, and I hurried after Carlson. I caught up with him in the corridor. "Excuse me, Lieutenant," I said.

He turned. "Sure. What is it?"

"I have an idea of who might've run down Glen Falconer."

"Oh?"

"Yes."

"You're thinking it wasn't an accident."

"Do you have a minute?"

"Sure. Go ahead."

I told him about Glen's trial and how Thomas Gall had threatened to "get" him and everyone else who he seemed to feel was responsible for the "not guilty" verdict. I told him how Paul Cizek had disappeared from his boat, and how I had seen Gall at Paul's house on Plum Island the next day. I told him that I believed Thomas Gall was carrying out his threat. I told him that Lieutenant Kirschenbaum of the Newburyport police was investigating Paul's disappearance.

Carlson leaned against the wall and listened, his eyes focused on my face. When I finished my story, he pulled a notebook from his jacket pocket. "Spell 'Gall' and 'Cizek' and 'Kirschenbaum' for me," he said.

I spelled the names for him, and he scribbled in his notebook. Then he looked up at me and said, "Falconer kills Gall's wife with a car, so Gall kills Falconer with a car. That's what you're thinking."

"Yes."

"An eye-for-an-eye sort of thing."

I nodded.

"Interesting," he said.

I shrugged. "It fits, doesn't it?"

"Easy enough," he said thoughtfully, "getting someone to take a look at this Gall's car. And I suppose somebody could check on where he was Saturday night."

"And where he was the night Paul Cizek went off his boat," I added.

"They didn't find a body, though, huh?"

"No. Not yet."

"It's been what?"

"A week ago Friday night."

Carlson shook his head. "Over a week, no body."

"I know. Anything could've happened."

"No body, no homicide," he said.

"At this point, they don't even know if there was a crime."

"Well," he said, "it sure looks like there's a crime here."

And if Glen Falconer died, I thought, it would be a homicide. Just as it had been when the woman Glen hit died.

It seemed too ironic to be a coincidence.

A half hour later Roger and I returned to the ICU. Brenda Falconer was seated in the waiting room with a magazine spread open on her lap. She was wearing a short blue skirt and a white blouse and high heels, and her hair was done up in an intricate bun, and she smiled quickly when she saw us.

I went to her and she held out her hand. I took it and said, "How are you doing?"

"Fine," she said, as if it had been a dumb question.

Roger sat two chairs away from her, folded his arms, and put his chin on his chest. Neither of them had acknowledged the other.

I stood there looking from one to the other, then said, "Well, I'll leave you folks to enjoy each other's company. I've got to run to the office. Let me know if there's any news, okay?"

"Sure," said Roger without looking up.

Brenda glanced sideways at him, then looked at me and nodded. "Thank you for coming," she said.

"You're welcome," I said.

18

I called Kirschenbaum at the Newburyport police station as soon as I got back to the office, and when I told him what had happened to Glen Falconer and how I thought Thomas Gall was making good on his threat to get revenge for the death of his wife, the lieutenant said, "Accidents *do* happen, Mr. Coyne."

"It's not hard to make something look like an accident."

"It's harder than you think, actually. Automobiles hit people on bicycles all the time. And we've investigated the Cizek thing pretty thoroughly, believe it or not. Now, I can't tell you whether he went overboard accidentally or on purpose. But we can't find a stitch of evidence that someone pushed him."

"If you had his body . . . "

"That could tell us a lot, sure."

"Isn't it unusual that his body hasn't washed up somewhere?"

"Well, yes, kinda."

"So don't you think *not* finding his body is a kind of evidence?"

He chuckled. "I get your drift, Mr. Coyne. Like the dog that didn't bark in one of those Sherlock Holmes stories. Sure. But that's a big ocean out there, and it's full of scavengers with sharp teeth, and tides and currents do funny things. I'll tell you the truth. I wish we had his body. But without it, and in the absence of evidence to the contrary, I'm pretty much inclined to believe Mr. Cizek had an accident. Accidents happen all the time."

"And murders don't?"

"Murders that leave no clues? Murders that are cleverly made to look exactly like accidents?" He laughed quickly. "Hardly ever."

"You released Paul's boat. Does that mean you've closed the case?"

"Mr. Coyne," said Kirschenbaum, "there was never any case to close. At least, not a police case. Without a crime, there's no case. We examined the boat. Looking for clues, like responsible policemen. The Coast Guard wanted to get rid of it, and it had nothing more to tell us."

"And the fact that Glen Falconer—"

"I'm trying to be patient with you," he said. "On account of you're a lawyer, and you're sincere, and you're really not too much of a pain in the ass. But I don't know what you want me to do."

"Somebody should talk to Thomas Gall."

"Sure. And every other individual who might've had harsh words with Cizek. You're right. One of 'em might've murdered him. And if we had evidence that there was a murder, we'd most likely interrogate every last one of them."

"Glen Falconer got run down, don't forget."

I heard him sigh. "I'll talk to somebody in Concord if it'll make you happy."

"Carlson," I said. "He's the Concord detective. Dick Carlson. I gave your name to him."

"I'm sure I speak for both Detective Carlson and myself," he said, "when I say thank you, Mr. Coyne, for all your help."

After I hung up, I lit a cigarette. I swiveled around to gaze out the window at the steel and glass and concrete of Copley Square. When I finished the cigarette, I picked up the phone. I pecked out half of Alex's number at the *Globe* before I replaced the receiver. I wanted to talk with her. I wanted to tell her what had happened to Glen. There might be a story there for her. It would interest her. We could discuss the implications. She could tell me whether I was crazy to think Thomas Gall was involved.

No. That's not why I wanted to call her. I really wanted to hear her say that she'd changed her mind. She'd canceled her lease on the post-and-beam home in Garrison, Maine. She'd decided not to take a leave of absence from the paper. She'd thought about it, and she'd decided she wanted things to stay the same. She liked it just the way it was. She liked how we took turns making dinner and how we played Trivial Pursuit, and although we kept our separate apartments, we slept together most nights and woke up together almost every day, and it was too perfect to change.

She wouldn't say that. If I called her, she'd be friendly and warm and she'd listen to my story about Glen and cluck sympathetically when I told her that the police were patronizing me, and we wouldn't talk about what was going to happen with us.

Alex wasn't going to change her mind, of course, and it was selfish of me even to wish that she might. If there was any mind-changing to be done, I'd have to do it.

I didn't know how much I could change.

I didn't talk to Alex all day. I wanted to call her, but I didn't. Even more, I wanted her to call me. But she didn't.

I knew she wouldn't be there when I got back to my apartment after work, and she wasn't. I heated up a can of Dinty Moore beef stew and ate it on the balcony.

I watched *Jeopardy* and tried to shout out answers before the contestants could. But I was slow and I felt stupid. Alex would've gotten most of them right.

At eight o'clock I snapped off the TV, went down to my car, and drove to Plum Island. I wanted to talk with Maddy Wilkins again. It was something to do. Better than spending a quiet evening alone in my apartment.

By the time I crossed the bridge to the island, the sun had set and the moon had risen. I turned left, crept down the narrow street, and then turned onto Meadowridge. I parked beside Paul's Cherokee, which was where Olivia and I had left it in the driveway.

The full moon lit the yard and the marsh out back, but the house was dark, and I felt a stab of disappointment. I realized I had been vaguely hoping that Paul would be there, and that he'd greet me at the door and offer me a beer, and we'd sit on his deck gazing out over the marsh and laugh at the big misunderstanding, and afterward I'd go home and call Alex and tell her all about it, and she'd laugh, too, and everything would be all right.

But, of course, everything wasn't all right. Paul was not there and Alex was moving to Maine.

I walked back to the street that ran the length of the island. Maddy had said she lived a couple of streets down, and I thought I recalled her waving her hand to the left. So I took a left. Short, sandy roadways similar to the one Paul lived on bisected this main street. The moonlight turned the sand white, and I walked down each of the little roads, and near the end of the third one I spotted an old yellow Volkswagen pulled up beside a cottage almost identical to Paul's. When I moved closer, I saw the bumper sticker that said, JUST SAY YO.

The house was ablaze with lights, and the bass throb of rock music thumped out of the open windows. I walked up to the front. A young couple were seated side by side on the steps. She had one arm slung across his shoulders. Both of them were holding beer cans, and they looked up when they saw me.

"Lookin' for Karen?" said the boy.

"Maddy," I said. "Maddy Wilkins."

He half turned his head and yelled through the screen of the front door, "Hey, Maddy! There's a guy here for you."

"Thanks," I said.

"No prob," he said.

After a couple of minutes, I said, "Um, maybe she didn't hear you? The music and all?"

"Why'n't you go on in," said the girl. "Maddy's in there somewhere."

I nodded. They edged over and I squeezed past them, pulled open the screen door, and went inside. The interior of the place was like Paul's, except that it pulsated with rock music I didn't recognize, and about a dozen young people were sprawled on the furniture and sitting cross-legged on the floor. Some were drinking beer and some held bottles of designer water. Their legs and fingers jiggled and twitched to the beat of the music, and not a single one of them was smoking dope.

Maddy was sitting on the floor leaning her back against a chair. The bearded young man in the chair was absentmindedly stroking her hair as he talked with the two girls sitting on the sofa across from him. It reminded me of the way Roger Falconer dangled his hand down to pet Abe and Ike, his retrievers.

I went over, and Maddy looked up. She frowned for an instant, then widened her eyes and smiled. "Oh, hi," she said.

"Hi, Maddy."

"Hey, want a beer or something?"

I shook my head. "I wondered if we could talk for a minute."

"Oh, geez, sure." She scrambled to her feet, came over, and took my hand. "Come on. It's too noisy in here."

She led me outside. We walked away from the music. She was still holding my hand.

"I remember you, but I forget your name," she said. "I'm pretty bad with names. I'm sorry."

"Brady," I said. "Brady Coyne. I'm—"

"I know. Paul's friend. Is that why you're here? You know something about Paul?"

I shook my head. "I'm afraid I don't. It's been over a week. I was hoping—"

"That I'd heard something?" She shrugged. "I haven't. It makes me furious, you know?"

"What does?"

"That he'd do that."

"You think—"

"That he killed himself? Yeah. That's what I think. He was a sad guy. Always moping around. I kept trying to cheer him up. You know, flowers and stuff. Some guys like flowers. But he was too far gone, I guess. I'd try to talk to him about making plans, doing stuff. You know, get him to think about the future? He'd just say, like, well, I'm not going to be here much longer. You know—"

"He said that?"

"What?"

"That he wasn't going to be here much longer?"

She nodded. "He said it more than once."

"As if he were going somewhere?"

She shook her head. "Well, that's what I thought. But it's pretty obvious what he really meant."

"That he was planning on taking his own life."

She squeezed my hand, then let go of it, hooked her arm through mine, and hugged it against her. "It's so sad," she said. "I go over every day to water the petunias. In this sandy soil, they need a lot of water. I keep thinking I should straighten up the place so it'll be nice for him when he gets back. But I know that's dumb. I mean, he's not coming back."

She continued holding my arm. I could feel her soft breast pressing against it. I gently pulled away. "Maddy, remember the man we saw in the street that day?"

"Sure. The big guy with the black beard."

"That's the one. You told me you'd seen him before."

"Yes. He was with Paul. They were sitting on his deck talking one night."

"You didn't hear what they were talking about?"

She shook her head. "When I saw that Paul had company, I just left. I mean, how was I to know who that man was? It might've been embarrassing if I'd walked up to them and sat on Paul's lap and gave him a big fat kiss, you know?"

"Is that what you usually did?"

"Sit on his lap and give him a kiss?" She smiled. "Sure. Geez." She cocked her head at me. "You're not, like, old-fashioned, are you?"

"Me?" I shrugged. "Sometimes I guess I am. I try not to judge things."

She shook her head. "I wish I knew what happened. The hardest thing is not knowing."

Olivia had said the same thing, I recalled. "So you don't know what they were talking about that night?" I said.

"Paul and that man?" She shook her head. "It looked like Paul was doing all the talking. I think he was angry."

"Paul was angry?"

"Yes. By the way he was sitting. Sort of tense and leaning forward. I didn't hear what he was saying, but I remember the tone of his voice, too. Like he was really giving it to him."

I took out my cigarette pack and held it to Maddy. She shook her head.

I lit one. "Have you seen him again?"

"That man with the beard, you mean?"

"Yes, him."

"No. Not since that morning when you were here."

We stood there in the moonlight. After a minute, Maddy said, "Why?"

"Huh?"

"Why did you come here tonight? Why are you asking me these things? Is something going on?"

"No, not really. It's just puzzling. He was my friend. Anyway, I just needed to get out of the house."

"Problems with the wife, huh?"

"Something like that," I said.

"Well," she said, "you should come on in and party with us. Cheer you up."

"That's very kind," I said. "But I don't think so."

"It'd be okay, you know. I mean, you being, um, older and all."

"Thanks, Maddy. Maybe another time. I've got to get going now."

She leaned against me, tilted up her face, and kissed my ear. "What is it with you older guys, anyway?"

"What do you mean?"

"You're all so sad."

"We are, aren't we?"

Maddy and I said good-bye, and I walked back through the moonlight to Paul's house. I found the key under the flower pot on the deck and went inside.

I turned on the light and looked around. Nothing had changed since I'd been there with Olivia a couple of days earlier. Dirty clothes still littered the floor. Magazines and newspapers were still strewn around the furniture. Mail was scattered over the top of the kitchen table.

It was the dwelling of a man with minimally developed nesting instincts. The cheap furniture probably came with the place. No paintings or photographs hung on the wall, no CD's or records crammed any shelves. There was no television or audio system. The few meals Paul ate here, I guessed, he either took out to the deck or gobbled over the sink. He obviously didn't sit at the table.

According to Maddy Wilkins, Paul had said he wasn't going to be around much longer. She thought he meant that he planned to kill himself.

People who intend to die soon don't bother building comfortable homes for themselves.

On the other hand, I'd lived in my apartment on the harbor for many years, and the spare bedroom was still full of unopened boxes and assorted junk. I tended to leave socks and newspapers strewn around the floor, just like Paul.

A calendar hung on the kitchen wall. The month of June featured black-and-white cows in a green pasture. Compliments of Skibbee and Fosburg Realtors.

I turned the pages back. Paul was not, evidently, a man who noted his appointments on wall calendars.

I started looking in one of the bedrooms. There was a single bare twin bed in the first one. On it were piled several fishing rods, a few tackle boxes, and a pair of rubber chest-high waders. Sweats and flannel shirts and foul-weather gear hung in the closet. Otherwise, the room was empty.

The medicine cabinet in the bathroom held razor blades, shaving cream, underarm deodorant, toothpaste, Rolaids, aspirin.

The second bedroom was evidently the one Paul used. There was a rumpled twin bed with the blankets thrown back. An alarm clock and a lamp and a paperback copy of *The Great Gatsby* sat on the bedside table. It had one drawer, which contained a bottle of aspirin, some coins, and the spare key to his car. It also contained a tube of KY lubricating jelly and a package of condoms. The tube had been squeezed several times and the condom package was almost empty.

I wondered what Olivia had thought, seeing that tube of "personal lubricant" and those condoms in there when she was looking for the car key, and again when she'd returned it to the drawer. Lieutenant Kirschenbaum had asked her if Paul was involved with another woman. Olivia, I recalled, had replied that she didn't know. But maybe she did. Maybe she'd known all along. Or suspected. Or didn't care.

Three medium-weight business suits, a couple of linen sport jackets, and several dress shirts hung in his closet, reminding me that Paul had been commuting to his office from this place. I rummaged through his clothes and found a sheer, lace-trimmed nightgown hanging among them. It was pretty apparent that Maddy—or somebody—had done more than sit on Paul's lap and kiss him. It didn't shock me.

I went back to the kitchen, sat at the table, and thumbed through Paul's mail, which, I inferred, Maddy brought in every day. No warning letters from would-be assassins, no ransom demands from kidnappers, no threats from blackmailers or clients or jealous boyfriends. Nothing personal whatsoever. No clues. Just junk mail and catalogs and magazines and bills.

I thumbed through the mail. There were two telephone bills and two bank statements, which I shoved into my hip pocket. Then I stood up, shut off the light, and went outside.

I was tucking the key back under the flower pot when something crashed against the side of my head.

19

I staggered forward and went down on one knee. Before I could shake the cotton batting out of my head, he was on me. A forearm clamped around my throat and bent me backward. I grabbed at it with both hands, gagging for air. It felt like a steel band crushing my larynx. White lights began to explode in my head.

Then, abruptly, he shoved me down and my throat was free.

I lifted myself onto my hands and knees, sucking in long gulps of air.

"Why're you doing this to me?" It was a low, harsh voice.

I turned. Thomas Gall was squatting there. In the moonlight his eyes glittered. His face was a shadow behind his bushy black beard.

I pushed myself up and slumped into one of the deck chairs. I rubbed my throat. "What are you talking about?" I said.

"If you don't leave me alone," he said, "I'll kill you."

"Mr. Gall," I said, "I've never even met you. I don't know what you're talking about."

But as I said it, I realized that I *did* know what he was talking about. I had mentioned him to both the Newburyport and the Concord police. I guessed that somebody, in turn, had mentioned me to him. I didn't figure he was clever enough to figure it out by himself.

I fumbled a cigarette from my shirt pocket and got it lit. I noticed that my hands were a little shaky, and the smoke felt harsh in my throat.

Gall stood up. He was a big man, taller than me and considerably bulkier. He held his arms away from his sides as if he had too many muscles to let them dangle straight down. He glared at me for a minute, then said, "Just get off my case, that's all. Okay? Get it? 'Cause I mean it. I'll kill you. I got nothin' to lose."

"I'm sorry about—"

He raised his fist. "Don't," he said quickly. "I don't wanna hear it. I don't wanna listen to you. You stay away from here, and you mind your own business, that's all. Understand?"

I nodded.

"I mean it," he said.

"I believe you."

He bent over and put his face close to mine, and in the moonlight I saw tears welling up in his eyes. He grabbed a handful of my hair. His mouth was twisting as if he were trying to speak. But no words came out. The tears began to overflow and dribble down into his beard.

Abruptly he let go of my hair. He straightened and held his hands up, palms outward, as if he were fighting against the temptation to hit me again. He stared down at me, then, without another word, turned and walked away. A minute later I heard the sound of an engine starting up, and I listened until it faded into silence.

I sat there on Paul Cizek's moonlit deck and finished my cigarette. Then I got into my car and headed back to Boston.

I didn't know whether to feel sorry for Gall or to fear him. Both, I decided. The man had lost his wife in a senseless, random way, and the person responsible for it had gone free. Grief combined with betrayal could make a man crazy.

When I got home, I found my apartment as empty as Paul's little cottage on Plum Island had been. The red light on my answering machine glowed steadily. No messages. Alex was not there, and she had not called me all day, and by comparison, my encounter with Thomas Gall somehow seemed trivial.

★ ★ ★

Since Alex had started spending a lot of time at my place, I'd tried to confine my littering of dirty clothes to the floor of my bedroom. The top of my kitchen table was generally cleared off now, because Alex liked to set places when we ate at it. I still left magazines and newspapers strewn on the coffee table and sofa. Alex did the same thing in her apartment on Marlborough Street.

I wondered what kind of a nest she'd build for herself in Garrison, Maine.

It was around ten-thirty. The same full moon that had lit up the sand on Plum Island shone down over the harbor. Alex would not be asleep yet. She had come over at ten or ten-thirty in the evening plenty of times. She loved to sit out on the balcony and watch the moon reflecting off the water.

It had only been yesterday that we'd driven up to Maine. It felt like it had been a very long time.

I was being stubborn and childish, waiting for her to call me.

I poured some Rebel Yell into a glass, dumped in some ice cubes, sat at the table, and dialed her number.

It rang several times before she answered.

"Did I wake you up?" I said.

"Oh, hi. No. I'm awake."

"How was your day?"

"Fine. Busy. You know?"

"Sure," I said. "Me, too."

I heard her chuckle.

"What?" I said.

"I didn't say anything."

"You laughed."

"Nothing, really."

"Is something funny?"

"If I laughed," she said, "it was not a laugh of humor. It was a small, wry laugh. The way one laughs at the ironies of life and the ways people try to deal with them."

"Listen," I said.

"What?"

I felt myself shaking my head. "Nothing."

We were silent for a moment. Then Alex said, "I'm sorry for making you sad."

"It's my problem."

"Yes, I guess it is. But when you're sad, I'm sad." I heard her take a long breath and let it out. "I can't *not* do this, Brady. If I didn't do this because I didn't want to make you sad, I'd always regret it. And I'd resent it. I'd resent you. Do you understand?"

"I want you to do it," I said. "It's not what you're doing. I'm happy for you. It's just me. I went to Paul Cizek's place tonight."

"Oh Brady . . . "

"No, listen. Back in the winter, he told me he was feeling discontented, unfulfilled. He didn't like the people he had to defend. I guess his marriage wasn't working. So what did he do? He left. He got himself a new place, a new life."

"And then—"

"I know. And then something happened. But my point is, he just did it. He made a change. I've got a lot more incentive than Paul had. To change my life, I mean. I've got you. So what's the matter with me?"

"It's hard, Brady. I think there's something wrong with people who do it easily."

"There's a beautiful full moon tonight," I said. "It's like daylight out there. You should see it on the water."

She chuckled softly. "I'm not coming over."

"I know."

"On September first I'm moving to Maine. I want you to always be in my life. So I need to know what you're going to do. That's all. When you figure it out, whatever it is, tell me. We'll take it from there."

"That's fair, I guess."

Neither of us spoke for a long minute. Then Alex said, "I'm sorry about the moon on the water. I bet it's pretty."

"It is," I said. "It would look a lot prettier to me if . . . "

"I know," she said quietly.

"Well, good night, Alex."

"Good night, Brady." She hesitated. "I'm glad you called."

"Me, too," I said.

I held the phone at my ear for a long moment after she disconnected. Then I hung up.

In a week it would be July. Then I'd have two months to decide what to do, to make my choice.

Or I could not decide. But that would be a choice, too.

Alex had already made her choice.

I got up and sloshed a little more Rebel Yell into my glass. I stood at the sliding doors and watched the moonlight dance on the water.

Then I went back to the table, lit a cigarette, and took Paul's phone bills and bank statements from my pocket.

Tearing them open felt vaguely criminal.

The first bank statement covered the period from April 15 to May 14. I recalled that Paul had moved to Plum Island sometime in March or early April.

There were just six canceled checks. One was for $476.27 to a bank in Virginia. A credit card payment, I guessed. To Skibbee and Fosburg Realtors, $1,200. Two months' rent, probably. One each for gas, electricity, and telephone.

The last check was made out to cash for $40,000. It was dated April 29.

Forty grand in cash. It left a balance of a little over $2,000 in his account.

There were five canceled checks in the second bank statement. One month's rent, $600; $329.40 for the credit card; the three utilities.

The monthly phone bills, for some reason, covered the period from the twelfth to the eleventh. The first one, from April 12 to May 11, itemized no calls. Nothing collect, no long distance, no credit card.

The second phone bill showed a cluster of long-distance calls between the fifteenth and twentieth of May. All to the 603 area code. New Hampshire.

One of the numbers had been called three times on three consecutive days. The rest had been called just once.

144

I wondered who lived at that number, and I wondered if that person had collected forty thousand dollars in cash from Paul Cizek, and if so, I wondered what it was for.

The next morning after Julie and I had reviewed the day's schedule, I gave her Paul's phone bill. "See if you can find out who lives at these numbers," I told her.

"Why?"

"Excuse me?"

"What's the point?"

"I don't know. I guess I want to know what happened to Paul."

"You think the answer is at one of these places?" she said, tapping her fingernail on the phone bill.

"Maybe. He apparently talked to several people in New Hampshire. Maybe he mentioned something to them. He took forty thousand dollars out of his checking account in April, then he made all these calls in May. He called one number three times in three days. Maybe he was paying somebody off or something. I don't know what I think right now."

"How do you want me to handle it?"

"Call the numbers. Talk to whoever answers. Don't mention Paul. See if you can get their names. Improvise."

"You mean lie."

"Sure. Lie. Make something up. Maybe you could be selling something. Lightbulbs. Newspaper subscriptions. Investments."

Julie grinned. "Sounds like fun. We haven't got anything pressing until eleven. We'll do it now. I'll go into your office. You stay out here and play receptionist."

"I can handle that."

She shrugged. "Maybe. It's not as easy as it looks."

She went into my office. I sat at her desk. I called Roger Falconer's number in Lincoln. His answering machine invited me to leave a message. I declined. Then I called Emerson Hospital. They connected me to the ICU. I identified myself as Glen's attorney, and a pleasant nurse told me that there was no change in his condition.

145

About an hour later, the phone rang and a button began blinking on the console on Julie's desk. I picked up the phone, depressed the button, and said, "Yes? Hello?"

"Geez," said Julie. "You're supposed to say, 'Brady Coyne, Attorney. May I help you?' "

"I'll never get it right," I said. "I'm just no good at this receptionist stuff. I guess I should go back to being a lawyer."

"Well, I'm awfully good at lying and wangling information out of strangers," she said. "Why don't you come in here?"

I went in. She had her feet up on my desk and a big grin on her face. I sat in the client chair across from her. "What've you got?" I said.

She touched the phone bill with the tip of a pencil. "I figured this number, the one he called three times in three days, might be the important one. But he called the other ones first, so that's what I did. I called them in the same sequence he did. There are six of them. He called four of them one day, two the next. Guess what?"

"Come on, kid. I don't know."

"All right. I checked the calendar. The first four calls were all made on a Sunday afternoon. See, it gives the date and time."

"And?"

"And the other two were the following morning. And guess what else?"

"Julie—"

"Okay. They're all real estate places."

I remembered how Alex had pored over the real estate classifieds in the Sunday *Globe*. I imagined Paul Cizek doing the same thing. "Peculiar," I said. "He'd already rented the place on Plum Island. What's he calling real estate firms for?"

"Well, I don't know," she said. "But I did find out that all these places are in Keene, New Hampshire. Except this number, the one he called three times. That's in Jefferson."

I nodded. "Okay."

"He made the first call that Tuesday. Then one on Wednesday and the last one on Thursday."

"Did you call it?"

146

"Of course. I said to myself, I bet this is also a real estate firm. Guess what?"

"Julie, for Christ sake, stop asking me to guess."

"I'm not asking you to guess. I'm just building the suspense."

"Consider it built. What'd you find out?"

"It's *not* a real estate firm."

I shrugged. "I don't get it."

"But it *is* a woman with a place to rent. And guess what?"

"Listen—"

"Sorry," she said. "The place has been rented."

"Could you find out when it was rented?"

"Yep."

"Sometime shortly after Paul Cizek called for the third time?"

"Bingo," she said with a snap of her fingers. "It's a summer place on a little lake. Very isolated. It's the only place on this lake. Comes with a rowboat, no outboard motor. Not winterized. She rents it monthly or for the season. May through September. Sleeps four comfortably. A couple of rollaway cots so you can squeeze in six. A nice little place for a couple or a small family to get away from it all. There's bass in the lake and a little swimming beach. Just four-fifty a month or two thousand for the whole season. That sounds pretty cheap to me."

"You learned all that?"

"Yes, I did."

"You're amazing."

"I know. I even found out where the place is located. Jefferson, New Hampshire, is about a half hour northeast of Keene. I told her that it sounded like just what we were looking for and we might want to rent it, but she said it was taken for the entire season, so I said we might be interested for next year, and she said why didn't we take a drive up there, check it out, and then we could call her back. She gave me directions. She said she didn't think the man who was staying there now would mind."

"A man is staying there now?"

"That's what she said."

"Jesus," I whispered.

20

Keene is tucked in the southwest corner of New Hampshire about equidistant from the borders of Vermont and Massachusetts. I'd been through it a few times, always on my way somewhere else, and I remembered it as a pretty little community, which, at around twenty thousand people, made it one of the most populous in the state. I figured the state college there inflated the population figure. When I checked the road map, I saw that no significant highway passed very close to Keene.

I located Jefferson an inch or so northeast of Keene. No red line on the map passed through it.

I left the office at four on Wednesday, went back to my apartment, changed into comfortable clothes, and joined the daily exodus from Boston at around a quarter of five. I slid a tape of Beethoven's Eroica Symphony into my cassette. It kept me company through all the traffic on Storrow Drive and Route 2 and ended around the time I reached the rotary in Concord. The Emperor Concerto took me from there to Keene, and I thanked Beethoven for the diversion.

The directions Julie had taken from the woman on the telephone were precise, and twenty minutes later I found the dirt driveway on the right, four-tenths of a mile past the barn with the rusty tin roof. It was marked by a slab of wood nailed to a pine tree with GALLAGHER hand-painted on it.

I turned onto the roadway, stopped, and got out of the car. The driveway sloped downhill through a meadow for a couple hundred yards, then disappeared into a pine grove. I could see the late-afternoon sunlight glinting off a ribbon of water beyond the pines.

I keep binoculars in the trunk of my car. I fetched them, then rested my elbows on the hood and scanned the place. I saw the outline of a cottage through the trees. Nothing else. No sign of movement or life.

I got back into my car and followed the rutted roadway down to the bottom of the hill. The cottage was tucked into the pines on the right. Vertical, unpainted cedar sides, a brace of big rectangular windows facing the pond, a brick chimney at one end, and an open porch across the front. An old Chevy pickup truck had been backed in behind it.

I pulled up next to the truck, got out, and stretched my legs. Nobody came out of the cottage to greet me, so I mounted the two steps onto the porch and knocked on the screen door. After a minute or so, I cupped my hands around my eyes and peered in through the screen, but I saw no sign of life.

"Anybody home?" I called.

After another minute, I decided nobody was home.

I wandered down to the pond and stood at the little sand beach. It was no more than fifteen feet wide, and about five feet into the water the sand stopped and the muck bottom began. A minimal swimming beach.

The sun was sinking toward the hills on the far side of the pond. It ricocheted off the water into my eyes. I used my hand as a visor and scanned the pond. I saw the silhouette of somebody in a rowboat coming around a point on the left, moving slowly toward me parallel to the shore. A long wake trailed out behind the boat on the glassy water.

I went back to the cottage. There were two sturdy rocking chairs on the porch, and I sat in one of them. The rhythmic clank of oarlocks echoed across the pond. Somewhere a crow cawed, and a chorus of bullfrogs grumped at each other. Swallows swooped over the water. Their wings ticked the surface here and there, leaving rings like rising trout.

The sound of the oarlocks grew louder, and then the rowboat appeared from around the corner. The bow crunched on the sand beach. Paul Cizek shipped his oars and climbed out. He stood there for a moment, shading his eyes, looking in my direction. Then he walked up to the cottage. He nodded at me. "Brady," he said. "It's you."

"Hello, Paul."

"So you found me."

"I guess I did."

He shook his head and smiled. He showed me the fly rod he was holding. "I've been doing it your way," he said. "Some nice largemouths in here." He leaned the rod against the wall. "Towards evening when it gets shady along the shore, they come to the surface for popping bugs. It's really a lot of fun."

He had bare feet and a half-grown reddish beard with gray streaks around his chin. He wore a pair of denim overalls over a black T-shirt. From behind his beard, he was grinning at me. "Come on in. Let's have a beer."

I got up and followed him inside. The description of the place the woman had given Julie over the phone had been generous. It was a single room with a ladder leading up to half a loft. A galley kitchen at one end, a woodstove at the other. A round table and four wooden chairs sat in front of a window with a view of the pond, and three raggedy sofas—convertibles, I assumed—occupied the rest of it. It was far less messy than the place on Plum Island. I figured Paul hadn't brought enough stuff with him to make a serious mess of it.

"Nice," I said.

Paul bent to the refrigerator, then turned and handed me a can of Budweiser. "We can sit on the porch," he said.

We went back out and sat in the rockers. The sun had sunk behind the trees, and the surface of the pond lay flat and dark.

"You don't seem surprised to see me," I said, watching the birds dart over the water.

"I heard your car coming down the hill. Sound travels clearly over the water. I knew it was somebody."

"I rather thought you'd be amazed at my canny detective work," I said.

"I give you more credit than that, Brady. You've done many cannier things than track me down. After it was too late, I realized I'd left my mail on the table. I figured the longer my body didn't turn up, the greater the chance that somebody would start snooping. I didn't think it would be the police. In the absence of a crime, they'd have no reason. It wouldn't be Olivia's style. But I know you."

"I'm the snoopy type."

"Yup. You like to know things."

"Well," I said, "now I know."

"If it had to be anybody," he said, "I'm glad it was you. So what are you going to do about it?"

"Do? I don't even know what I know. All I know is, you're here. You didn't fall off your boat." I turned to him. "But you tried to make it look that way."

He shrugged.

"Olivia's a wreck, you know."

"I figured she would be. She'll get over it."

"She'll be relieved—"

"No," he said. "You can't tell her."

"That's not fair."

"Trust me, Brady. It's fair."

"You'll have to convince me of that, my friend."

"It's really simple. This was the only way I could make a clean break. I tried the Plum Island solution. It didn't work. I couldn't get away from anybody or anything. Old man Tarlin had me involved in a bunch of cases that I couldn't gracefully pull out of. Olivia was hurt and confused. I realized there was no half measure. I had to find a way to start over again." He sighed. "I told you last winter, Brady. I was heading for a crack-up. Since I've been here, I'm a new man. Paul Cizek is dead. I guess this makes no sense to you."

"Actually, it does make sense," I said. "I've been thinking of making some changes myself. But I doubt if I'd fake my own death to accomplish it."

"Don't knock it unless you've tried it."

"You've hurt a lot of people," I said quietly. "There has to be a better way."

"You think it's a cop-out, huh?"

I nodded. "I guess I do."

"Well," he said, "it's what I'm doing, and I can't help what other people think." He hesitated, then said, "Are the police investigating my—my disappearance?"

"No, I don't think so. Not actively, anyway. You're missing at sea, as far as they're concerned. Some day your body may wash up somewhere."

"Good," he said. "That's good."

"But I've got to tell Olivia, Paul. She's hurting."

He shook his head. "No way. If she knows, she'll be hurt and confused for the rest of her life. I expect now she's grieving. Fine. She'll get over that. I'm dead. Out of her life. It's done, and it's final, and she'll move on."

"I'd be irresponsible not to tell her."

"You'd violate my trust if you told her. You're my lawyer."

"I'm her lawyer, too."

"Since when do you tell one client's secrets to another client?"

"You put me in a tough spot," I said.

"No. You put yourself in a tough spot by coming up here. As your client, I forbid you from telling anybody what you found out today."

"Shit, Paul."

"Think about it."

"I guess I'll have to."

"All you've got to do is forget it and leave me alone. It's really simple. Consider me dead. Don't screw things up for me."

152

"It may be simple," I said, "but it's not easy."

"It *is* easy. Just don't do anything."

I thought of Alex. She was moving to Maine. I had to decide whether to go with her. "You're wrong about that," I said to Paul. "Choosing to do nothing is still a choice. Not telling Olivia would be very hard. It would be lying."

"It would be preserving our confidential secret. That's different."

"How about another beer?" I said.

"Sure." He got up and went inside, and a moment later he returned. He handed me another Bud. "I generally go to bed when the sun sets," he said. "I read for awhile. I go to sleep easy, and I sleep soundly, and I wake up with the birds. I put on some coffee and go for a swim, and then I come back and have a mug or two on the porch and watch the sun come up. I'm doing a little writing. Some of my old cases have given me short story ideas. I don't think they're very good yet. But I'm practicing. I row around the pond every afternoon. I practice my fly casting, or sometimes I just drift and dangle a worm over the side and catch enough perch and bluegills for a meal. I chop wood. I walk through the woods. Once a week or so I take the truck to the store and get some groceries. Nobody sends me mail. I pay for everything with cash. There's no telephone or computer or television. Just a little radio that gets a PBS station." He shrugged. "I'm trying to cut my life closer to the bone, that's all."

"Simplify, simplify," I said.

"Thoreau," he said. "Sure. Old Mister Midlife Crisis himself. I've been reading *Walden* as I sit here listening to the birds and smelling the pines and trying to stop frittering away my life in details. Henry showed us the way."

"Hole up in a cabin in the woods."

"Why not? That's what he did. He made a convincing case for it."

"Well," I said, "I do know some things about quiet desperation. I just don't see how you can run away from it. But if you can carry it off, good luck to you."

"I *can* carry it off, Brady. You're the only one who can spoil it for me."

"I'll think about it," I said. I gazed at the pond for a few minutes, then said, "Maybe you can answer a question for me."

"Maybe," said Paul.

"Is it Thomas Gall you're running from?"

"Gall?"

"Don't pretend you don't know the name."

"Oh, I wasn't." He sipped from his beer. I thought he wasn't going to answer me, but after a long silence, he said, "How'd you find out about Gall?"

"I didn't find out anything, really. Just that he'd visited you on Plum Island."

"He did," he said. "We got some things straightened out."

"The man threatened to get you."

"Well, as you can see, he didn't."

"He threatened me, too," I said.

Paul turned to me. "Huh?"

"A couple nights ago. At your place, when I found your telephone bills."

"He was there?"

I nodded.

"What'd he do?"

"He hit me. He grabbed me by the throat. He said if I didn't leave him alone he'd kill me." I shrugged. "That's all."

Paul chuckled.

"That's funny?" I said.

"No, not really. I was just thinking. You probably figured Gall had dumped me off my boat. You thought he was a desperate murderer. But, as you can see, he didn't do anything to me. Don't be afraid of Gall. He's all ripped up inside. But I don't think he's gonna kill anyone."

"He might've already," I said.

"Huh?"

"Glen Falconer's in the hospital."

"Falconer? What happened?"

"Hit and run. He was riding a bicycle."

"A bicycle?"

"Yes. He'd given up driving cars because he couldn't give up drinking. Someone ran him down last Saturday night. He's in bad shape."

"He was driving his bike while he was drunk?"

"I guess so."

Paul snorted. "That's pretty fucking funny."

"You think so?"

"Sure. In an ironic sort of way. Another vehicular homicide, DUI. Except now the drunk's the victim. And he's riding a bike."

"Irony isn't always funny," I said.

"Valid point," said Paul. "So you think it was Gall?"

"It makes sense, doesn't it?"

"Maybe it does," he said. "Still, I wouldn't worry about Gall. He's a mess. Anyone would be in his situation. If he ran down Falconer—well, I can see that. But he won't hurt you."

"I'm vastly comforted," I said.

We sat in silence. The darkness that had filled the woods was seeping out into the clearing in front of the cottage. After awhile, Paul got up and went inside. He turned on a lamp. Its light filtered out the windows onto the porch. It cast shadows around the cottage and made the sky look black.

From behind the screen door, he said, "Another beer?"

"No. I've got to drive home."

"Why not stay for supper? I'll fry up some potatoes, open a can of beans."

"I've got to get going. Thanks anyway."

Paul came back out and sat beside me. We were silent for a few minutes, then he said, "What're you thinking, Brady?"

I shrugged. "Nothing, really. I guess I'm just glad to know you're alive."

"Yeah, I'm alive."

I turned to him. "How are you really, Paul?"

"I'm healing." He smiled. "It's slow. I'm working on it. Good days and not-so-good days. It was good to see you, Brady."

"It was good to see you, too," I said.

"Don't come back, though, okay?"

"I wasn't planning to."

"Nothing personal."

"I understand."

I got up and went to my car. Paul followed.

"I almost forgot," I said. "I've got a message for you."

"You can't." He grinned. "I'm dead."

"Eddie Vaccaro says he needs you."

"Vaccaro?" He hissed out a quick breath. "I'm not what that son of a bitch needs."

"He thinks the Russo family's got a contract on him. He wants to go into the witness protection program."

"Did you advise him to go to the feds?"

"Of course. But he wants you. You're the only one he trusts."

Paul laughed quickly. "I hope Russo gets him."

"He thinks pretty highly of you."

"It's hardly mutual. It was defending guys like Eddie Vaccaro that made me fall out of my boat." He hesitated for a moment, then said, "Vaccaro went to you, huh?"

"Yes. He showed up in my office last week."

"Fuck him," said Paul softly. "You absolutely must not tell him anything."

"I won't," I said. "But I want to tell you, Eddie Vaccaro is a very scary guy. He made me take a fee so he'd be a legitimate client and I'd have to protect his confidentiality. I think he would've shot me in the eye if I'd refused."

"Yeah," said Paul. "He probably would've."

21

Charlie was waiting at our regular table at Marie's when I got there a little after noon on Friday. He was sipping coffee and peering through his reading glasses at some legal-looking papers, and when I pulled out the chair across from him and sat down, he looked up and said, "Where've you been?"

I looked at my watch. "I'm five minutes late."

He nodded. "Exactly. You're late."

"Shit, Charlie."

"Do the math, Coyne. Five minutes is a measurable percentage of your lifetime. You shouldn't waste it."

Charlie McDevitt is the chief prosecutor for the Boston office of the Department of Justice. He's also my old Yale law school roommate, fishing and golfing partner, and best friend. We help each other out from time to time in exchange for a lunch at Marie's. Usually it's Charlie who helps me and I'm the one who pays for the best non–North End Italian food in Boston.

But this time he'd invited me to lunch. I assumed he wanted something.

"Sorry I kept you waiting," I said. "But you're usually not so damned crabby about it. What's up?"

He took off his glasses, folded them, and tucked them into the inside pocket of his suit jacket. He slid the papers into his briefcase, which sat on the floor beside his chair. Then he put his elbows onto the table, rested his chin on his clasped hands, and looked at me. "Eddie Vaccaro," he said.

"What about him?"

"Exactly. What about him?"

"Is that what this is about?" I said. "Here I am, thinking my old pal wants to buy me lunch, talk fishing, reminisce about our days in New Haven, tell a few jokes, and what it really is, he wants to play quiz games with me."

"A week ago Wednesday," said Charlie, "at one-thirty-seven P.M., Edward R. Vaccaro, a killer in the employ of Vincent Russo, who, as you probably know, the Feebs have been trying to nail for years, entered a certain one-man law office in Copley Square. He emerged at four-forty-two. As you undoubtedly also know, a couple years ago this Vaccaro, who makes a pretty decent living by shooting people in the eye with a twenty-two–caliber automatic pistol, refused to testify against Russo, even when given the opportunity to exchange an almost certain life term in a federal penitentiary for immunity from prosecution and life membership in the witness protection program. He went to trial and, *mirabile dictu,* a clever Boston defense attorney managed to outmaneuver a contingent of federal prosecuting attorneys. Vaccaro went free. No testimony. No Vincent Russo."

"Charlie—"

"Very embarrassing," he said. "It looked like a lock. We assumed somewhere in the course of the trial, Vaccaro and his smart lawyer would see the light and come across for us."

"Paul Cizek," I said, "being the smart lawyer."

"And your client, right?"

I shrugged. "You know better, Charlie."

"Sure, okay. Client privilege."

"You don't have to tell me about Vaccaro," I said. "I know who he is."

"I'm sure you do," said Charlie. "You probably also know why he spent over three hours in your office nine days ago."

"I do," I said. "How'd you know he was there?"

"How do you think?"

"Oh, sure," I said. "He's being followed."

"Yes. And the reports come to me. And when I read that he appears to be lining up a new attorney, I figure something's afoot. And I want to know what it is. So when this new attorney happens to be the one guy who—"

"Charlie," I said. "Please don't."

"Vaccaro's a cold-blooded killer," said Charlie. "And Vinny Russo's not exactly your Mr. Rogers, either. He gets kids hooked on drugs. He pays money to have people murdered. He lures young girls into prostitution. He—"

"You don't have to tell me this," I said.

"How do you think it looks?" he said. "Vaccaro hires Cizek, refuses our deal, and Cizek gets him off. Then Cizek, who's your client, turns up missing, probably dead. And then Vaccaro shows up in your office? And it just happens that you are my best friend?"

"I don't know what you're thinking," I said, "but whatever it is, it's wrong."

Charlie sat back and shook his head slowly. "I'm sure it is, Brady. I don't like what I'm thinking. I want you to straighten me out."

"I wish I could."

"Meaning what?"

"I met with Vaccaro for about twenty minutes. I will not meet with him again. But for reasons that you should be able to infer, I can't tell you what we talked about."

"You accepted a fee from Eddie Vaccaro?" Charlie shook his head.

"Charlie, shit—"

He held up his hand. "I can imagine how it was, Brady. He's a frightening man. I don't blame you."

"Believe me, Charlie—"

"Forget it," he said. He cocked his head and peered at me. "This has something to do with Paul Cizek's death, doesn't it?"

"Tell you what," I said. "Let's order lunch. Then I'll tell you something. How's that?"

"You'll actually tell me something? Wow."

"Don't, Charlie. You know you can trust me."

He nodded. "I always thought I could." He looked around, lifted his hand, and a moment later one of the BU undergraduates who Marie hires to wait tables came over.

Her name was Ellie, and she wore a gold stud in her nose and a gold cross around her neck. She told us she was a physics major with a minor in music and an ambition to go to law school. Charlie told her the law was a fine profession, and I didn't contradict him.

Charlie ordered the cannelloni, and I settled on the antipasto for one.

After Ellie left, I said, "I can tell you that Vaccaro wanted me to deliver a message to Paul Cizek. I can't tell you what that message was."

"Wait a minute," said Charlie. "Didn't Vaccaro know that Cizek had died?"

"He didn't seem to believe that Paul was dead."

"And that's why he went to you? Because he thought Cizek was still alive?"

"Seemed peculiar to me," I said. "At the time."

Charlie sat back and stared at me for a moment. Then he nodded. "At the time," he repeated. "You've learned something since then."

"I wish I could talk about it."

Charlie began nodding. "Cizek isn't dead, is he?"

"If I'd known what was on your mind today," I said, "I'd have refused to meet with you."

"Paul Cizek is alive, and that's another secret you can't share."

"Let's talk about fishing."

"He's your client," said Charlie. "So you can't tell his wife, and you can't tell his law firm, and you can't tell me."

"We should try to get to the Farmington this weekend," I said.

"Or maybe head out to the Deerfield. We haven't been trout fishing all spring."

Charlie smiled and nodded. "Sunday. Let's do it."

"We'll talk baseball and mayflies. I've got some woman problems I'd like to tell you about. We'll play blues tapes in the car. All professional subjects strictly verboten."

"Agreed," he said. "On Sunday we'll avoid sensitive legal topics. But—"

He looked up as Ellie delivered our lunches. After she left, he took a bite of his cannelloni, smiled, and mumbled, "Mmm."

I speared an anchovy from my antipasto. "Can we change the subject?"

"I'd sure love to know why Eddie Vaccaro wants to see Paul Cizek," he said.

"I think it's a moot question."

"Why? If Cizek's alive—"

"I didn't say he was alive."

Charlie took another mouthful of cannelloni. "A week or so ago," he mumbled, "we arrested a guy at Logan Airport because he had a homemade bomb in his carry-on luggage. Crude thing. Couple sticks of dynamite, wires, battery. Probably wouldn't have even worked. Still, a terrorist is a terrorist. Big federal offense, of course, taking bombs onto airplanes. We read him his rights, and he refused counsel. Turns out he works in a bookstore in Salem. Bachelor. Lifelong Republican. A deacon in the Episcopal church."

"Classic terrorist profile," I said.

He smiled. "I talked to him. He didn't seem to understand that he'd done anything wrong. Claimed he had no intention of detonating it, or using it as a threat to hijack the plane, or anything like that. Said he just felt better having it with him. I said, 'How could having a bomb on an airplane make you feel better?' He said he hated to fly. He had this terrible phobia that a terrorist would blow up the plane. I said, 'If you're so afraid of bombs, how come you tried to bring one aboard?' And this guy looks at me with these innocent, puppy-dog eyes and tells me, he says, 'I called up the airlines and I asked them what were the odds of there being a bomb on the plane. About a million to one, they said. So I thought about that,' he says, 'and then I asked what the odds were of there being two bombs on the same plane. Infinite, was the answer. There'd simply never be two separate bombs on the same plane. It wouldn't happen.' "

"Charlie, wait a minute," I said.

He lifted his hand. "Listen. The guy is looking at me. 'Now do you see?' he says. And I admit that I don't. So he says, 'It's simple. If *I* bring a bomb aboard, I'm safe.' " He spread his palms and grinned.

"That's a pretty funny story," I said. "What's your point?"

"Does there have to be a point?"

"There usually is," I said. "So what're you trying to tell me?"

Charlie shrugged.

"If you think too much, you twist simple things around until they seem complicated. Is that it?"

"That would work," he said.

"I'm not going to tell you what Eddie Vaccaro and I talked about."

"I know. You already said that."

"Justice may be simple to you," I said.

"Basically, it *is* simple. It's making sure that people who commit crimes are punished."

"No," I said, "it's much more complicated than that."

"Lawyers are the ones who make it complicated. The law is simple."

"So why don't you just talk to Vaccaro?" I said. "Ask him what we talked about? It seems to me that would be the simple thing to do."

"Yeah," said Charlie. "We'd like to."

"So . . . ?"

"But last night our guys lost him."

"He gave them the slip?"

Charlie nodded.

"Well," I said, "here's something I can tell you. I don't know where he is."

"Yeah, but Paul Cizek might know."

"I can't help you there," I said. "Sorry."

"Yeah," said Charlie. "Me, too."

22

Charlie and I agreed to meet in the parking lot of the Papa-Razzi restaurant on Route 2 in Concord at seven on Sunday morning. We still called it "the place where the Howard Johnson's used to be," although the old HoJo's with the orange tile roof had been gone for several years. We'd leave my car there and take Charlie's four-wheel-drive van, and we'd be on the banks of the Deerfield River by nine. In June there are insects on the water, and trout feeding on them, all day long. Sulfur-colored mayflies, tan caddisflies, a few stoneflies. We'd fish till dark. We'd make a day of it.

We would discuss no business. When Charlie and I played golf we sometimes discussed cases or clients or judges or legal theory. But we had agreed a long time ago that trout fishing is too important, and requires too much concentration, to corrupt with business conversation.

When I got back to my apartment that Friday evening, I heated a can of beans and ate them directly from the pot at the kitchen table while I flipped through the current issue of *American Angler*. Then I wandered around the place, assembling my trout-fishing gear. We weren't going until Sunday, but I wanted to have it all ready. It took me a couple of hours to find everything and to decide what to bring with me and to pile it all neatly beside the door.

Then I sprawled on the sofa and turned on the television. My old black-and-white Hitachi gets only five channels, two with considerable fuzziness, and on this Friday evening in the middle of June I found three sitcoms, an old John Wayne movie, and, on Channel 2, a show on home repair. I left it on Channel 2. A man in a beard was demonstrating the art of laying hardwood floors.

Even when I lived in a suburban house with Gloria and my two young sons, I had never contemplated laying a hardwood floor.

I was, of course, trying very hard not to think about Alex, and the fact that she wasn't with me, and that this was the first Friday evening in almost a year that we hadn't been together, and that I was facing the first weekend in that amount of time without her.

Trying not to think about her, of course, didn't work. I might as well have hung a big sign on the wall that said: DON'T THINK ABOUT ALEX.

I held out until a little past ten. Then I switched off the TV, poured two fingers of Rebel Yell over some ice cubes, lit a cigarette, took a deep breath, and called her.

She answered on the first ring with a cautious "Hello?"

"It's me."

"Oh, geez," she said. "I was going to call you."

"You were?"

"It's Friday. You're there and I'm here. It doesn't feel right."

"No," I said. "It doesn't."

"I was screwing up my courage," she said.

"If I'd known that, I'd have waited. I was very nervous, calling you."

"Nervous?"

"I was afraid you wouldn't want to talk to me," I said.

"Oh, Brady . . . "

"You know what I think?" I said after a moment.

"I wish I did," she said softly.

"I think that not seeing you is confusing me. It's not helping me to clarify things. Not seeing you makes me feel as if the only important thing is being with you, that nothing in my life matters except that. It makes me want to just chuck it all and go to Maine with you. It makes me want to ignore all the other variables. Not seeing you makes this big hole in me where you belong, and it hurts, and it needs filling, and the simplest thing would be just to go with you. Except it's not simple."

"I know," she said.

"I could think more clearly if that hole weren't there."

"Do you think so?"

"Yes."

"I do want you with me, you know."

"Sure," I said. "I know that."

"You have talked a lot about changing your life. You know, the Montana dream. Simplifying. Focusing on important things."

"I have talked about those things, I know."

"I think you've been serious about it."

"I think I have, too. But I'm not sure. I've got to figure it out."

"My moving is forcing you to do that."

"If you weren't moving," I said, "I might never do anything. I might just glide along the same way, year after year, until I was too old to do anything. It's good that you're moving. It's forcing me to think."

"Well," she said, "do you think you'd like to have company?"

"Now?"

"Is it too late?"

"Hell, no."

"I'll be there in an hour."

Her cheek rested on my shoulder and her fingers played on my chest. Her bare leg pressed against mine. I stroked her hair in the dark.

"If I kissed you ever so gently," she whispered, "you wouldn't think I was trying to manipulate you or influence any decisions you had to make, would you?"

"No. That would be small-minded and foolish of me."

I felt her mouth move on me.

"Or," she murmured, "if I touched you—there, like that—you wouldn't misconstrue my motives?"

"No. Definitely not."

"Or—mmm—if I did this . . . ?"

"Jesus, no, Alex. Of course not."

When I woke up, Alex was gone, and the hole in my stomach had returned. She had brewed a pot of coffee, and a note was propped against it. It read: "Call me. A. XXOO."

Alex worked on Saturdays. She got up at seven, while I was still asleep, showered, and slipped out without waking me up. She spent all day Saturday in her little cubicle at the *Globe,* hunched over her word processor, polishing her Sunday feature. Every Saturday.

Come September, she wouldn't be doing that anymore.

Eight or nine more Saturdays. Then things would change.

Around noon I called the Falconer house in Lincoln and found Roger at home. Glen's condition had deteriorated. He'd been unconscious for nearly a week. There had been some encouraging signs on Thursday. He'd moved one hand and mumbled. Then his coma had deepened. Now there were indications of kidney distress. I asked if there was anything I could do. No, Roger said. There didn't appear to be anything anyone could do. Brenda was there. She was a comfort, he said.

As far as he knew, the Concord police had made no progress in finding the hit-and-run driver, Roger said. They'd promised to tell him if and when they did.

I called Alex at one, when, I knew, she generally took a break. Her recording invited me to deposit a message in her voice mailbox.

"It is I," I said. "If you're—"

"Mmm," her unrecorded voice mumbled. "H'lo."

"Pastrami on rye?"

"Corned beef on wheat, actually," she said. "With a big fat dill pickle."

"How's tonight?"

"Sure. Let's go out and celebrate."

"Celebrate what?" I said.

"Independence Day."

"That's not for another week."

"Our independence, I mean."

"Independence from what?"

"Convention. Expectation. The humdrum and the mundane. The slings and the arrows. The tumult and the shouting. The agony and the ecstasy."

"Oh," I said. "That stuff."

We ate in one of the upstairs dining rooms at the Union Oyster House. We had Bloody Marys and Alex ordered baked finnan haddie and I had oyster stew, all in the two-hundred-year-old tradition of the Oyster House.

I wanted to tell her all about Glen Falconer's bicycle accident and my visit from Eddie Vaccaro and my confrontation with Thomas Gall. A lot had happened in the week we'd been apart. I wanted to brag about how I'd tracked down Paul Cizek, and how I'd found him emulating Thoreau on a little New Hampshire pond, trying to live deliberately, to front only the essential facts, to suck out all the marrow of life, to drive life into a corner and reduce it to its lowest terms.

I also wanted Alex to know that I didn't envy Paul. Beneath his brave talk of simplicity, I sensed that he had not really escaped the quiet desperation that had sent him fleeing in the first place.

I couldn't tell Alex about Paul Cizek, of course. She was a reporter, and I was a lawyer bound by law and ethic to protect my client's secrets. Anyway, if we'd talked about Paul, we'd have ended up talking about me, and my own quiet desperation, and how a little post-and-beam home on a dirt road in Maine could work the same as a cabin on a pond.

Simplify, simplify.

Sure. Easier said than done.

★   ★   ★

Sunday morning at six o'clock it was my turn to slip out of bed while Alex was still sleeping, brew a pot of coffee, and prop a note against it. "Love you," it said unoriginally. I added several *X*'s and *O*'s.

It was a glorious Sunday in June, and Charlie and I fished from a little after nine in the morning until dark, and all the way to the Deerfield and back, and during our frequent time-outs, when we sat on streamside boulders to listen to the river and watch the trout feed on insects, we did not once violate our sacred agreement to avoid all topics relating to the business of the law.

We fooled some trout, and some trout fooled us. Neither of us fell in. A perfect day of fishing. We stopped for burgers and beer at a roadside pub in Charlemont.

During the long ride home in the dark I talked about Alex, how she was moving to Maine at the end of the summer, and how I was afraid I'd lose her, and how tempting it was to go with her.

All Charlie said was "Change is hard, Brady. Either way, it's hard."

I dropped him at his car in Concord and it was nearly midnight when I pulled into the parking garage under my building.

I sat behind the wheel for a moment. It was late and I was tired, that healthy fatigue that comes from a long day of wading in a cold river and fly casting in the sunshine and fresh air. The yellow fluorescent lights of the garage cast odd shadows on the concrete pillars and the rows of parked vehicles, and through the half-opened car window I heard the soft echoes of water dripping somewhere.

I sighed, got out of the car, retrieved my fishing gear from the backseat, and headed for the elevator. I was reaching to push the button when I felt something hard ram into the back of my neck.

"Don't turn around," came a raspy voice I didn't recognize from behind me.

"You got it," I said.

"Drop your stuff."

I let my rod case and waders and fishing vest drop to the floor.

"Okay. Over there. In the corner."

He shifted the gun barrel to my back and used it to prod and steer me around the side of the elevator shaft into the dark corner beside a parked minivan.

An arm went around my chest, pulling me back against a man who I sensed was bigger and bulkier than I. The gun barrel left my back for a moment. Then it was pressed against the corner of my right eye.

"Jesus Christ," I mumbled.

"Shut up," came the voice, so close to my ear I could smell the tobacco and garlic on his breath. The pressure of the gun barrel made my eye ache.

"You're not Vaccaro," I said.

"Nah. I don't shoot guys in the eye like that weasel. I shoot 'em in the back of the head. Civilized, you know?"

"Can you move the gun, then?"

He chuckled. "Sure. Whatever you say." The gun left my eye and jabbed into the base of my spine. "That better?"

"Yes. Thank you."

"Where's Vaccaro?"

"Is that what this is?"

"My uncle needs to talk to him."

"I don't know where he is. I hardly know him. I—"

The gun barrel rammed into my side. "Don't bullshit me, pally. He was in your office the other day."

"Yes. But that was the only time, and he didn't tell me where he was going. I have no idea where he is."

"So what did he say?"

"He just said he was looking for his lawyer. Not me. A friend of mine. He thought I might know where he was. But I didn't."

"That's it?"

"That's it."

"What else?"

"Nothing."

The man hugging me against him was silent for a moment. Then he said, "Uncle tells me to bump you, that's what I do. Right? This time he says ask you questions polite. So I do that. I do what my uncle says. You telling me the truth, no problem. Okay?"

"Okay."

"Uncle finds out you're lying . . . "

"I hear you," I said.

"We got an eye on you," he said. His arm moved away and then the pressure from the gun barrel in my back was gone. "You stay right here for awhile. Got it?"

"Yes."

"Five minutes."

"All right."

I heard his feet moving on the concrete floor, and I listened until the echoes faded and died. I took a deep breath, hesitated, then turned. The parking garage was quiet and eerie and empty. I went to the elevator, gathered up my fishing gear, and rode up to my sixth-floor apartment.

I flicked on the lights and dropped my gear onto the floor. "Alex?" I called.

There was no answer. I went into the bedroom. She wasn't there. I sat on the edge of my bed, and that's when I noticed that my hands were trembling. I fumbled a cigarette, got it lit, and dialed Charlie's number on the phone by the bed.

It rang five or six times before he answered.

"It's Brady," I said.

"Christ, I just spent a whole day with you. I just got into bed. I'm pooped."

"Charlie . . ."

He hesitated, then said, "What is it? What's this I hear in your voice?"

"I just had a gun stuck into my eye by someone who was looking for Eddie Vaccaro."

"Oh, man . . ."

"He said—"

"Vinny Russo," said Charlie.

"He didn't say. He mentioned his uncle."

"That'd be Vinny." Charlie paused. "You met one of Russo's thugs. Look, Brady, you don't know where Vaccaro is. Hell, nobody knows where he is. They're just checking out all their possibilities. Okay?"

"I didn't like it at all," I said.

"No. But I don't think you need to worry."

"Ever had a gun stuck in your eye?"

"No. Listen, Brady. They've got no reason to hurt you. They don't hurt people for no reason. Understand? That's not how they operate."

"I lied to him," I said. "I didn't tell him that Vaccaro wanted to turn himself in to you."

Charlie chuckled. "You didn't even tell me that."

"I'm telling you now."

"We already knew that, Brady. I'd guess Russo knows it, too. It's no secret. That's why everyone's looking for him."

"So . . ."

"So you've probably got nothing to worry about."

"Probably? Shit, Charlie."

"Don't worry. Nothing's going to happen. Go to sleep."

"Fat chance," I said.

Eventually I did get to sleep. It took a while. When I woke up, the sun was shining and the fear I'd felt down there in the gloomy, mid-night shadows of the parking garage had faded. Only a tender bruise near the base of my spine reminded me of my encounter with Vinny Russo's hired thug.

I spent Monday in court and ran into my old friend Judge Chester Popowski in the lobby afterward. When I told him about my adventure in the parking garage, Pops insisted on buying me a drink. He echoed Charlie's advice. I had nothing to worry about, he said, and he made me believe it. By the time we parted it was too late to go back to the office. It was another beautiful June–almost-July afternoon, so I walked all the way home from East Cambridge to my apartment on the harbor.

I found myself glancing back over my shoulder from time to time. Nobody seemed to be following me.

I got there around six. Alex was on the balcony munching an apple. Her shoes were off and her bare feet were propped up on the railing and she'd hiked her skirt up over her knees. Her glasses were perched on top of her head and her face was tilted to the sky and her eyes were closed. I kissed the side of her neck.

Without turning or opening her eyes, she reached up and touched the side of my face. "You're all sweaty," she said.

"I walked all the way from the courthouse."

"Good for you. Gonna join me?"

"Let me change and get an apple of my own."

I did, and when I sat beside her and propped my own heels on the railing next to hers, she reached for my hand and said, "I drove up there yesterday."

"To the—your place in Maine?"

"Yes."

"Why?"

She took her hand away and ran it through her hair. "I just wanted to see it. To see that it was real. To see if it was the way I remembered."

"And?"

"I love it. It's perfect. And it makes me sad."

"Alex—"

She turned, leaned toward me, and kissed my mouth. "Let's not talk about it," she said. "We've already said everything." She stood up and threw her apple core out into space. We watched it arc down to the water. The splash it made on impact was barely visible from my balcony.

She rubbed her hands together, then smoothed her skirt against the fronts of her thighs. "I bought salmon steaks and fresh peas and baby potatoes," she said. "You stay here and relax. I'm cooking."

Darkness was seeping into the apartment and Alex and I were patting our stomachs and sipping coffee at the table when the phone rang. I didn't move.

"Aren't you going to answer it?" she said.

"No. I'm too comfortable. Let the machine get it."

After the third ring, the answering machine in the corner of the living room clicked on, invited the caller to leave a message, and then beeped.

"Oh, Brady," came Olivia Cizek's voice. "Oh, Jesus. You've got to be there. Please answer."

I got up quickly and picked up the wall phone. "I'm here," I said. "What's up?"

"It's Paul . . . "

"Yes."

"He—I talked to him. He wants to see us."

"Us?"

"Yes. You and me."

"When?"

"Now. Tonight."

"I can't do it tonight, Olivia. I've got company."

"I know you talked to him," she said. Her breath seemed to catch in her throat, and I guessed that she was crying. "He told me everything. I—he's frightened. He sounds—I don't know. Desperate. I don't—"

"All right," I said. "I'll pick you up. I'll be there in half an hour."

"Please hurry," she said.

I hung up the phone. Alex was sitting with her elbows on the table and her chin propped up on her fists, staring out the window. I went over and stood beside her. "I've got to go out," I said.

She nodded without looking at me.

I squeezed her shoulder. "It's Olivia Cizek," I said. "It has to do with Paul. I'll explain later. I'm sorry."

She pressed her cheek against my hip. "It's okay. Go take care of business."

"Will you be here when I get back?"

"I don't know."

23

The traffic was light, and I pulled up in front of Olivia Cizek's house on their suburban side street in Lynnfield a little after nine-thirty. Before I could set the emergency brake, the passenger door opened and she slid in.

"Let's go," she said.

I pulled away from the curb. "Can you tell me what's going on?"

"What's going on is Paul's alive after all and he's somewhere in New Hampshire and he's in some kind of trouble. He said you knew how to get there."

"Yes. I found him. I couldn't—"

"I know. He told me. He made you promise not to tell me."

"I'm sorry."

"It's all right. Please. Just hurry."

Olivia sat there staring straight ahead. I drove fast. I tried to start a couple of conversations, but she made it clear she didn't want to talk. After a while I slid a tape of Bach's first two Brandenburg Concertos into the player.

An hour and a half later I passed the barn with the rusty tin roof. I found the "Gallagher" sign and turned onto the long dirt driveway that wound its way down to the pond.

The two big windows on the front of Paul's cabin threw a pair of pale yellow parallelograms onto the pine needles. Otherwise the darkness was complete in the thick grove of pines. I pulled up in front, and before I could turn off the ignition Olivia had opened the door, jumped out, and run over to the cabin.

I got out of the car just in time to hear her scream.

She was kneeling on the ground with her head bowed as if she were throwing up. Her fingers were clawing at the pine needles. Her breath came in long, gagging shudders.

I started toward her. "Olivia," I said. "What—?"

She stood, ran to me, and threw her arms around me. "It's him," she said. "It's—oh, God."

I looked over her shoulder and saw Paul.

He was sprawled on the ground in the shadow of the porch, face-down, with one arm reaching into one of those yellow rectangles of light. The pine needles all around his body were wet and shiny with blood.

I held Olivia tight. She lifted her head, looked blankly at me for a moment, then buried her face against my chest. Her fingers dug into my back. Her shoulders heaved.

As my eyes adjusted to the darkness, I could see that Paul's side from neck to waist was drenched with blood. He was wearing the same overalls and T-shirt he'd had on the day I'd visited him, and his feet were bare, and his body looked shrunken in his clothes.

"He's dead," she whispered. "Oh, Jesus. Somebody killed him. He's dead." She was shuddering against me, and I held her close.

And then I realized that whoever had done this to Paul could still be around, lurking in the shadows, fully prepared to do to me and Olivia what he had done to Paul. "We've got to get away from here," I said.

"But what about . . . ?"

"We can't help him. Come on. Let's go."

"Shouldn't we cover him or something?"

"We've got to leave him that way. For the police."

She nodded. "Yes, of course."

I put an arm around her waist and helped her stumble back to the car. I opened the passenger door and guided her inside. Then

I went around the other side and slid behind the wheel.

I turned around and headed back up the dirt road. Olivia huddled against the door, hugging herself.

I drove back the way we'd come. I remembered a little mom-and-pop store at a crossroads a couple of miles before we'd come to the barn with the tin roof. There had been a pair of gas pumps out front and a Coke machine beside the door and hand-printed signs advertising live bait and cold beer. I thought I recalled seeing a phone booth.

The phone booth was there. I pulled up beside it and got out, leaving the motor running and the headlights on. I told the officer that I was reporting what I thought was a murder. I started to try to give directions, but when I mentioned the "Gallagher" sign he said he knew where the Gallagher cottage was. He asked me my name and told me to meet him at the top of the driveway.

I got back into the car. "The police are coming," I told Olivia.

I headed back to Paul's place.

"I thought he was dead," Olivia whispered. "Then he called. And he wasn't dead after all. And now . . . "

I couldn't think of anything to say to her.

I turned onto the driveway and stopped. A minute or so later a police cruiser with its blue light flashing pulled up beside me. The window went down and a cop leaned out. "Follow us," he said.

We drove down to the cottage. Two uniformed officers got out. One of them went to the cottage and played a flashlight over Paul's body while the other one came over to my car. Olivia and I were sitting inside with the windows open, and he rested a forearm on the roof, bent down, and asked if we were okay. We both nodded.

"You folks wait right here," he said.

After a minute, the one with the flashlight went back to the cruiser. I could hear him speaking into the two-way radio, and I heard the crackling voice of a dispatcher. Then he came over to join us. "They're on their way," he said, and he joined his partner in leaning against my car to wait.

A few minutes later I heard sirens in the distance. Their wail grew steadily louder, and then a line of headlights appeared on the hillside, weaving its way down through the trees to us.

First came another cruiser, followed by a rescue wagon and two unmarked vehicles. Three EMTs hopped out of the wagon and jogged over to Paul's body. A man in a sport jacket opened the passenger door and said, "If you'll come with me, please, Miss." He took Olivia's elbow and led her to his sedan. A guy wearing a suit with no necktie introduced himself to me as Lieutenant Capshaw. I accepted his invitation to follow him over to his car. We sat in the front seat. He kept the door open, and the dome light illuminated the inside of the car and made the outside seem darker. I related the events of the evening, beginning with Olivia's phone call to me and ending with my phone call to the police.

When he asked me if I could think of anybody who might be inclined to kill Paul Cizek, I said, "Yes. Several people."

I told him about Thomas Gall, who had threatened Paul in court and who I had seen twice at Paul's place on Plum Island.

I told him about Eddie Vaccaro, who was looking for Paul and who certainly was capable of blowing away a man who crossed him. Or maybe one of Vinny Russo's gunmen, trying to use Paul to find Vaccaro.

I even mentioned Roger Falconer. The old man might have found a way to blame Paul for what had happened to Glen. Anyway, Roger hated Paul.

Capshaw kept nodding and taking notes, and when I paused, he said, "How would any of these people find him? He was hiding out up here, wasn't he?"

"Paul might've contacted one of them," I said. "Anyway, *I* found him. I guess someone else could, too." I hesitated. "Shit," I said. "Somebody could've followed me up here the other day. I could have led Paul's killer to him. This could be all my fault."

Capshaw nodded. "So it could," he said. Then he turned to me. "You didn't do it, did you?"

"Me?"

"You and her." He jerked his head in the direction of the other sedan, where Olivia was having her own conversation with a police officer. "The wife. You and the wife."

"No," I said. "We didn't do it."

He shrugged. "I was just asking. Better to confess up front, you know?"

"Sure," I said.

"You two weren't—you know, having an affair?"

"No."

"What about her?"

"What do you mean?"

"Think she did it?"

"Lieutenant," I said, "for one thing, I am Olivia's attorney, so if I did think she did it, I wouldn't tell you."

He looked at me for a minute. "What's the other thing?"

"The other thing is, I don't think she did it."

"She could've, you know," he said. "She could've come up here, blasted him, driven home, called you, and brought you up here to witness her grief when she saw the body."

"That's interesting," I said.

He shrugged.

"If she's a suspect," I said, "I should be with her."

"If or when she's a suspect, you will be, Mr. Coyne." He paused. "Unless you are, too, of course."

They were photographing Paul's body where he lay on his belly. The flashes lit up the pine grove like summer lightning. Then they zipped Paul up in a black body bag and loaded him into the wagon.

They took Olivia and me to the police station in separate vehicles. They assured me someone would be following along behind in my car.

Capshaw took me into his cubicle, gave me coffee in a Styrofoam cup, and questioned me all over again, this time with a tape recorder. He asked me the same questions and I gave him the same answers. Then he thanked me and led me out into what resembled a small hospital waiting room, with plastic chairs and a stack of frayed magazines on a table. I smoked a cigarette and drank coffee and ignored the magazines.

After a few minutes, Olivia came out with her interrogator. She stood in front of me, rubbing her hands together as if they were cold. "They want me to identify his body," she said.

"Jesus," I said. "You shouldn't have to—"

"It's okay," she said. "It's got to be done."

It was a fifteen-minute drive to the little country hospital. Olivia and I sat in the back of a police cruiser. The two officers who had been the first to arrive at Paul's cabin sat in front. Neither of them spoke for the entire ride, either to each other or to us.

They led us inside. I waited with one of them in the lobby while the other took Olivia to an elevator.

I asked the cop if it would be okay for me to go outside for a cigarette. He shrugged and followed me out. We leaned against the building.

"Rough one," he muttered.

"It's her husband," I said.

"Don't know how they can expect her to look at him. I never seen such a mess. Looked like both barrels of buckshot from about ten feet. The whole side of his head was blown away. Shit."

I turned to look at him. He was staring down at the ground, shaking his head slowly back and forth.

We were still standing there when Olivia came out. She was holding onto the policeman's arm. She looked blankly at me, then gave me a small nod. "We can go home now," she said quietly.

It was after three in the morning, and the New Hampshire back roads were empty. Now and then we passed a house where a single downstairs window glowed orange, and I imagined a farmer or a milkman or a fisherman sitting at his kitchen table drinking coffee and getting ready for his day.

I had turned off the tape deck. Olivia said nothing, and I didn't try to talk, either. After a while, her breathing became slow and rhythmical and I figured she was sleeping.

About the time I turned onto Route 2 heading east, Olivia cleared her throat, and in the darkness she said, "The wedding ring and the watch. I gave him the watch on our fifth anniversary. The ring's inscribed with our initials and the date we got married. I had the watch inscribed, too. It says, 'Stand by your man.' It was a joke. They had taken the ring and the watch off him, and they asked me if there was any way I could positively identify them. I told them what the inscriptions said. And then they asked me if I'd be willing to look at his body, and I told them I'd try. They had put a towel or something over his face and chest and said I didn't have to look if I didn't want to, and I didn't. I couldn't. But they'd removed his clothes, and I told them I didn't need the ring or the watch. I slept beside that body for almost ten years."

"I'm terribly sorry, Olivia" was all I could think of to say.

"No, it's all right, Brady." I felt her hand touch mine on the steering wheel. "It's not your fault."

"Maybe if I'd told you—"

"Shh," she said. "He made you promise not to. You did the right thing."

"I might've believed suicide. He seemed very depressed when I saw him. Struggling with it. Looking for answers. Hiding out in a cabin in the woods."

"Yes. He'd been depressed for a long time."

"He quoted Thoreau to me," I said. "The reason Thoreau went to Walden was to get away from everything and sort things out. His brother had unexpectedly died. Thoreau was probably pretty depressed, too, although you don't get that in his writing."

"Nobody murdered Thoreau," said Olivia.

24

The sky was turning silver when I pulled into Olivia's driveway, and when I turned off the engine I could hear the mingled twitters, chirps, and squawks of several different species of suburban birds greeting the new day. They were dissonant and arrhythmic, like an orchestra warming up, but beautiful and comforting, too.

Olivia sat beside me looking at her house.

"Is there somebody who can stay with you?" I said to her.

She nodded. "Oh, sure."

"Look . . . "

She turned to me. "I'll be okay, Brady. I accepted the fact that he was dead once. I guess I can do it again."

"If there's anything I can do . . . "

"I know. Thank you." She leaned to me and kissed my cheek. Then she opened the car door, slid out, and closed it softly behind her. She walked up the path to her front door and went inside without looking back at me.

By the time I got to my apartment, the sun had risen above the harbor and was streaming through the glass doors. I slid them open and sprawled in one of the aluminum chairs on the balcony. I closed my eyes and felt the warmth of the sunlight and the salty cool of the sea breeze wash over my face. My eyes burned and my head ached and my stomach sloshed with acid and adrenaline, and I couldn't figure out whether to make coffee or go to bed.

Bed, I decided. I prepared a pot of coffee and set the timer for eleven. Then I called the office, and when the machine answered I told Julie that I'd had an all-nighter, that I'd explain when I saw her, that I'd try to be in by noontime, and that she'd have to reschedule anything I had for the morning.

Then I went into my bedroom. The shades were drawn, and it was cool and dark in there. I shucked off all of my clothes and crawled in naked.

And only then did it occur to me that Alex was not there. She had decided not to stay. She hadn't even left me a note with X's and O's on it propped against the coffee pot.

I lay awake longer than I'd expected to, trapped in that fuzzy place between consciousness and sleep. I thought that if Alex had been there in my bed, all warm-skinned and languid and mumbling, and if I could have held her against me with my chest against her back and my belly pressed tight against her bottom and my arm around her hip and her breast in my hand and her hair in my face, then maybe those pictures of Paul's dead body lying facedown on the pine needles would have stopped flashing in my brain and I'd have fallen asleep much more easily.

It was nearly one in the afternoon by the time I got to the office. Julie looked up at me, grinned, and said, "You look like roadkill."

"Compared to my usual bright-eyed, incredibly handsome self, you mean," I said, trying to smile and doing a poor job of it.

"No. Compared to anybody." She cocked her head and looked at me. "What happened? Wanna tell me about it?"

I nodded.

"Another all-night orgy?"

"You flatter me," I said. "I haven't had an all-night orgy since college." I sighed. "No, this was not a fun night."

I sat beside her desk and started to tell her about it. When I got to the place where Olivia found Paul's body lying on the pine needles, Julie murmured, "Oh, that poor woman," and I remembered the tube of KY lubricant and the half-empty package of condoms beside Paul's bed in the Plum Island cottage. I thought of telling Julie that Paul had apparently been screwing Maddy Wilkins. But I didn't see what difference that made. Paul was still dead and Olivia still mourned him. So I left that part out, and about halfway through my recitation, she slapped her forehead and said, "That reminds me. Lieutenant Horowitz called. He said it was important. I almost told him he could get you at home. You better call him."

"I didn't finish my story."

"It's an awful story," she said. "I'm not sure I want to hear the rest of it."

"I want to tell it to you. But I guess I better call Horowitz first."

I went into my office and dialed Horowitz's number at the state police headquarters at 1010 Commonwealth Avenue.

"Horowitz," he growled when the switchboard connected us.

"Coyne," I said.

"Our colleagues in the Live-Free-or-Die state ask us to pick up a couple guys they want to interrogate, and when I inquire as to what the fuck it's all about, they mention a homicide and damned if your name doesn't pop up. So maybe you can shed some light on it for me."

"Thomas Gall?" I said.

"Yup. And Eddie Vaccaro."

"So did you pick them up?"

"We got Gall. Haven't tracked down Vaccaro yet. I guess we're not the only ones trying. The feds are looking for him, too. But we're doing the neighborly thing. It's New Hampshire's problem, and they've got no obligation to explain it all to us. Still, Paul Cizek used to be a helluva prosecutor, and then he became a big pain in the ass as a defender. But he was always an okay guy, and more or less a friend of mine, and when my friends get murdered it kinda bothers me, and when I'm asked to pick up people who might've done it, I get curious. So talk to me."

I told Horowitz everything. I began back in November when I

persuaded Paul Cizek to take Glen Falconer's case, and I told him how Paul had seemed depressed and confused when he'd miraculously gotten Glen off, and how Thomas Gall had threatened everybody connected with Glen's shocking not-guilty verdict, including the jury and the judge and, of course, Paul Cizek, the defense attorney, and Glen himself. I told him how soon thereafter Paul had left his wife and moved to Plum Island and then, a few months later, disappeared, and how I'd run into Gall when I went to Paul's place, and how Maddy Wilkins had told me that she'd seen Paul and Gall together. I told Horowitz how I'd tracked Paul down in New Hampshire, where he'd seemed edgy and still a little depressed and, in retrospect, frightened. I told Horowitz about my unsettling visit from Eddie Vaccaro and my subsequent, and even more unsettling, encounter with Vinny Russo's thug, and I told him how Glen Falconer was run down by a hit-and-run driver, and how Paul had been killed, and that I thought it added up to Thomas Gall avenging the death of his wife and the injustice that had been done in court.

When I finished talking, Horowitz was quiet for a moment. Then he said, "Yeah, okay. Makes sense." Then he hung up.

I held the dead telephone in front of me. "You're welcome," I said to it.

Sometime in the middle of the afternoon I called Alex's number at the *Globe*. Her recorded voice invited me to leave a message.

"It's me," I said. "If you're upset, I want to explain. I didn't get back until about six this morning, and there's no logical reason why you should have waited all night for me, and I don't blame you for leaving. But I was sad that you weren't there. It's important for me to know what you were thinking and why you didn't leave me a note. A note with an *X* and an *O* on the bottom would've reassured me, and I probably would've gotten to sleep quicker. As it was I lay there with a million random thoughts colliding in my head, thoughts about you all mixed in with thoughts about Paul Cizek, who, as you probably know by now, we found murdered in New Hampshire, and I don't know why I'm rambling on like this except I am feeling especially lonely, which death always tends to do to me, especially the death of a friend." I took a deep breath. "I love you. Call me, okay?"

I waited at the office until after six, but Alex didn't call. Maybe she's going to surprise me, I thought. She'll be waiting at my place when I get there. She'll have her feet up on the rail of the balcony with her skirt bunched up around her waist. Or maybe she'll be curled in the corner of my sofa, wearing my baggy sweatpants and watching the evening news. She'll be eating an apple or sipping from a bottle of beer, and there'll be a pot of lentil soup simmering on the stove.

But she wasn't there. The red light on my answering machine glowed steadily. She hadn't called, either.

Around eleven the next morning, Julie buzzed me. "Mr. McDevitt on line two," she said.

I pushed the blinking button. "What's up, Charlie?"

"Eddie Vaccaro," he said.

"What about him?"

"My guys found him."

"Well, good. The state police are looking for him, too."

"They already know," he said. "He was propped up in the backseat of a ninety-three Buick Skylark in the parking garage at Logan. There was one bullet hole in his left eye and another behind his right ear."

"Oh, shit," I said.

"Shit, indeed," said Charlie.

25

On Wednesday morning I sat in a conference room in the federal office building in Government Center with Charlie and two of his fellow prosecutors, one male and one female, and talked into a tape recorder. I told them what Eddie Vaccaro had told me as well as I could remember it—that he believed his boss, Vincent Russo, had a contract out on him, that the hit man was terrified that he was going to get hit himself, that he was prepared to give testimony against Russo in exchange for immunity and a slot in the witness protection program, and that he trusted only Paul Cizek to negotiate it for him. I told them what I had told Vaccaro—that I didn't know where Paul was, that as far as I knew he'd gone overboard and drowned, and that he should retain another lawyer.

I told them about having a gun stuck in my eye in my parking garage.

I told Charlie and his friends that a week after my session with Vaccaro I had found Paul Cizek living in a cabin on a pond in New Hampshire and that I told Paul that Vaccaro was looking for him.

A few days later Paul Cizek was murdered. "And now Vaccaro's dead," I said.

"Cizek was murdered Monday, right?" said Charlie.

"Yes," I said.

"Okay," said Charlie. "That's it." He gestured to the young man and young woman who had been sitting with us. "Leave us alone for a few minutes."

After they turned off the tape recorder and left the office, Charlie leaned toward me. "They found Vaccaro's body early yesterday morning," he said. "Tuesday. The ME tells us he'd been dead between twenty-four and thirty-six hours."

"That would be—"

"Sunday night sometime."

"About the time I got a gun in my eye in my parking garage."

Charlie nodded.

"Which means—"

"It means Vaccaro died before Cizek, for one thing," he said. "So he couldn't've killed him."

"It also means he might've been dead when that gorilla was asking me where he was."

"Yep," said Charlie.

Vaccaro's body, said Charlie, had been noticed by a young couple returning from a vacation in Portugal. The Buick Skylark was parked beside their Honda in a dark corner of the third level of the airport parking garage.

Cause of death had been one of the two .22-caliber hollow-point slugs fired from close range into his brain—one through the left eye, the other through his skull, just behind his right ear.

"That was Vaccaro's trademark, of course," Charlie told me. "The left eye and behind the right ear. The eye was always the first one. When Vaccaro killed a man, it was always with a message from Vinny Russo, the man who paid him. Eddie wanted his victims to see exactly what was happening to them. Make sure they got Vinny's message. So he gave them a bullet in the eye. Whoever hit Vaccaro was obviously delivering a message, too."

The Skylark was registered to Vaccaro's wife, whose name was Marie and who lived in Malden. The steering wheel, door handles, dashboard, and vinyl upholstery had been wiped free of fingerprints, although the technicians had found some partials on the frame that matched Vaccaro's and some smudges that might've belonged to somebody else.

There were bloodstains on the backseat where the body had been lying, but they found no skull fragments or brain tissue in the car, suggesting that the actual shooting had happened somewhere else.

They found no murder weapon, no note, no matchbook or cigar butt or lost wallet in the car. No clues at all, obvious or microscopic.

"The absence of clues," said Charlie, "being an important clue, of course."

"A professional hit," I said.

"So it appears."

"That's what he was afraid of," I said, "and that's what happened."

"And there goes Vinny Russo," said Charlie. "Down the tubes. And now we've got to try to find the guy who hit Vaccaro, and we'll offer him immunity, and see if we can't get him to give us Vincent Russo. Uncle Vinny knows this, of course. So he'll hire someone to hit the hit man before we catch up with him, and so it goes, round and round. Next time a professional killer shows up in your office, why not have Julie give me a call, huh?"

"I doubt if it'll happen again," I said.

Alex wasn't there when I got home that afternoon. I hadn't expected she would be. I changed into jeans and sat on my balcony. I smoked and stared at the sky. I thought of Eddie Vaccaro and Glen Falconer—one dead, the other close to it. And I thought of Paul, of course. He was dead, too.

I thought of Vinny Russo sending his henchmen out to find and kill a man who might've already been dead.

My mind kept switching back to Alex. I contemplated the ephemeral nature of youth and happiness and love and life itself.

Images of Alex kept transforming into Olivia and Maddy Wilkins. Paul had apparently been screwing Maddy. If so, Olivia must have suspected. She couldn't have missed seeing the evidence in the drawer of Paul's bedside table when she retrieved his car key and again when she put it back.

Where did Thomas Gall fit into this equation? A sad, grieving, perhaps desperate man. But a murderer?

Eddie Vaccaro, of course, was a murderer. But he died first. So he couldn't have killed Paul.

The pink afterglow of the sunset still tinged the sky over the Plum Island marsh as I pulled in behind the yellow Volkswagen with the JUST SAY YO bumper sticker.

I mounted the steps of Maddy's cottage. The inside door was open, and amplified guitar music came at me through the screen door. Jimi Hendrix, if I wasn't mistaken. I rapped on the door frame and called, "Maddy? Are you there?"

A minute later she appeared on the other side of the screen door. She was holding a can of Diet Coke. She wore a plain blue T-shirt and pink shorts. She squinted at me through the screen. "Hello?" she said uncertainly.

"It's Brady Coyne," I said. "Paul Cizek's lawyer?"

"Oh, sure." She pushed the screen door open. "Come on in."

"I need to talk to you," I said. "Can you come outside?"

She glanced over her shoulder, then turned back to me and said, "I guess so. Want a Coke or something?"

"No, thank you."

She came out and we sat on the front steps. "What's up?" she said.

"I want to ask you a couple of things, Maddy. It's very important that you tell me the truth."

"Oh, wow," she said. "Like a cross-examination, huh?"

"Yes. It's actually possible that the questions I ask you could be asked of you in court, under oath."

"I haven't done anything wrong."

I flapped my hands and shrugged.

"Are you trying to scare me?"

"No. I just want you to tell me the truth."

She hugged herself. "You *are* scaring me. What's going on?"

"I'll explain," I said. "First, I want you to remember everything you can about the man with the black beard who we saw the first day I was here. You know who I mean?"

She nodded. "I already told you everything. He was at Paul's place a couple of times. I saw them one night talking out on his deck." She shrugged.

"Did you hear what they were saying?"

She shrugged. "I don't know. I don't remember."

"It could be very important. Please try."

She squeezed her eyes shut for a moment. Then she opened them and looked at me. "Well . . . "

"Yes?"

"I wasn't spying on them."

"I know, Maddy. I'm not accusing you of that. What did you hear?"

"I didn't realize that other man was there when I went over. I didn't mean to sneak around, but I was barefoot, and it was dark, and I guess they didn't know I was there. I heard voices out on his deck, so I went around the side of the house, and when I saw that Paul was with somebody I stopped so they wouldn't see me. Paul was . . . he said something like 'Play it my way' to that man. And the man kind of nodded, and Paul said, 'Trust me.' "

"Are you sure that's what he said? 'Play it my way'?"

She nodded. "Maybe not those exact words. But something like that, because I remember wondering what they were planning to do. I do remember him saying 'trust me.' It struck me as pretty strange."

"What else, Maddy? Did either of them say anything else?"

She looked at me and shook her head. "Nothing. I left. It was obviously a private conversation."

"Did Paul ever mention that man to you?"

"No. Never."

"And you didn't say anything to him about seeing them together?"

"Oh, no."

"Can you remember anything else?"

"Not really. I hung around by the end of Paul's street, waiting for the man to leave, and after awhile the two of them came out and walked to where the man's truck was parked. They shook hands and then the man drove off and Paul went back to his place."

"They shook hands."

"Uh-huh."

I paused to light a cigarette. Then I said, "Okay, Maddy. Just one more question, okay?"

"I still don't understand—"

"I'll explain, I promise. First, I want you to tell me about you and Paul."

"What about us?"

"Were you lovers? Were you sleeping with him?"

She let out a long breath that could have been either a laugh or a sigh. "Is that a crime?" she asked softly.

"No," I said. "But lying about it might be."

She was shaking her head. "I liked to pretend," she whispered. "I had such a wicked crush on him. I told my friends that I was sleeping with him, that he loved me, that he'd promised to marry me as soon as he got his divorce. Half the time I believed it myself. He was so nice to me, it was easy to think he really loved me. I wanted to take care of him. I wanted to hold him and kiss him and make him happy. He was so sad and tense all the time. I *knew* I could make him feel better." She turned to me, and I could see tears glittering in her eyes. "You know what I mean?"

I nodded. "I know about love, yes," I said. "Are you saying that you and Paul never slept together?"

"Not even close," she said softly. "He treated me like a daughter, not a lover. He took me on his boat a couple of times. He let me cook for him. He liked to talk to me about my future and my career and stuff like that. One time he kissed me on the top of my head. That was the closest we ever came. I mean, he already had someone anyway. It was stupid of me to—"

"Someone else?"

"Sure."

"Another woman, you mean?"

She nodded. "She was there a lot. Whenever I saw her car there I'd get this twisted-up feeling in my stomach."

"Did you ever see this woman?"

"Oh, yeah." She smiled quickly. "I—I kinda spied on them a couple times."

"What did she look like?"

"She dressed rich. You can tell expensive stuff, even if it's just a skirt and a blouse or something. She seemed very sophisticated, and she was beautiful. Tall, thin, blond. It made me sad, you know? Next to her, who was I? I knew I could never compete with a classy lady like that."

"Her car was parked there, you said?"

"Yes."

"Do you remember what the car looked like?"

"Sure. It was a really neat little white sports car. A two-seater. A Mercedes convertible."

26

"**M**addy," I said, "I've got to use your telephone."

"Sure, but—"

"I've got to make a call. It's important."

She shrugged. "Okay. Come on in."

Jimi Hendrix had stopped singing, and a young woman was sprawled on the sofa eating yogurt from a cardboard container and reading a magazine. Maddy pointed to the telephone on the wall in the kitchen, then stood there watching me.

"I need privacy, Maddy," I said.

"Huh? Oh, sure." She went over and sat with her friend on the sofa.

I glanced at my watch. It was a little after nine. I pecked out the number for Horowitz's office at state police headquarters. Horowitz wasn't there. I asked to be patched through to him and apparently managed to make a convincing case for it.

I waited a few minutes, and then Horowitz said, "This better be damn good, Coyne."

"I think it is," I said. "Or pretty bad, depending on how you look at it."

"I don't need any fucking riddles. What do you want?"

"I want you to tell your counterparts in New Hampshire to fingerprint Paul Cizek's body."

"Why?"

"To identify it, of course."

"Yeah, why else?" He paused. "Wait a minute. That body's already been ID'd, hasn't it?"

"Mrs. Cizek identified it, yes."

"Then—?"

"Lieutenant," I said, "I could be wrong. If I am, I'm sorry. But if I'm right, then that body doesn't belong to Paul Cizek."

"I thought you saw it."

"I saw a body," I said. "It was facedown."

"You mean you never . . . ?"

"No."

He was silent for a moment. "No shit?"

"No shit."

"I think you better explain, Coyne."

"If I'm right, I will. If I'm wrong, you'll be too mad at me to care."

"You got that right, pal," he said. "Okay. I'll get back to you."

After Horowitz and I disconnected, I dialed Roger Falconer's number in Lincoln. Brenda answered.

"It's Brady Coyne," I said. "I need to talk to you."

"Okay. Go ahead."

"I think it would be better in person."

She hesitated. "When?"

"As soon as possible. It'll take me at least an hour to get there. Make it ten-thirty."

"What's this all about, anyway?"

"You and Paul Cizek."

She was silent for a moment. Then she said, "Yes. All right." She paused. "I don't think you should come here."

"I agree. You tell me where."

"How about the Colonial Inn in Concord? Meet me on the front porch."

"I'm on my way," I said.

Brenda was sitting in one of the rockers on the front porch of the Colonial Inn, gazing out over the village green. She was wearing tight-fitting jeans and a sweatshirt with a picture of Wile E. Coyote on the front of it, and she was smoking a cigarette.

I'd never seen her in jeans, and I'd never seen her smoking, and I'd never have pegged her as a Wile E. fan.

I realized I barely knew her.

I took the rocker beside her. "I wanted to talk to you before the police did."

"I haven't committed any crime," she said quietly.

"No," I said, "but several crimes have been committed, and I suspect you can shed some light on them."

"I don't see how." She flipped her cigarette away, then turned to me. "Sure, I was sleeping with Paul. Frankly, I don't much care who knows it. Roger might be upset, but Glen's beyond understanding or caring. Actually, Glen's been beyond understanding or caring for years."

"I'm certainly not judging you," I said.

She angled her head and stared at me for a moment. Then she nodded. "Okay. Good. Then I don't know what you want. It's a simple story, see? Glen's a drunk, and drunks don't seem to have much interest in other people. They love their booze, not their wives, and you can forget sex, because drunks don't, um, function. Paul Cizek was a sexy guy, and he wasn't a drunk. He was separated from his wife. We hit it off. We were attracted to each other. Very attracted." She spread her hands. "Then he disappeared, and that was that."

"You never heard from him after that?"

"I assumed he fell off his boat and drowned."

"He didn't. He faked it. He was living in New Hampshire."

Both of her hands went to her mouth. "That bastard," she whispered.

"Did you ever talk to him about Glen?"

She nodded. "Sure. He talked about Olivia and I talked about Glen. I guess that's what adulterers mainly talk about. Their spouses."

"Did you tell him how Glen had given up driving cars and was riding bicycles around the back roads at night?"

"Sure. We laughed about it."

"Did Paul seem unusually interested in it? Did he ask questions about it?"

She narrowed her eyes. "Oh, Jesus," she said. "I know what you're thinking."

I waited, and a moment later she said, "Paul asked me a lot of questions about Glen. He wanted to know when he went out on his bike, the roads he took, the places he went to. It seemed like—you know, pillow talk." She fumbled in her bag and came out with a cigarette. I took out my Zippo and lit it for her. She took a long drag and exhaled it out there on the porch of the Colonial Inn. The pale glow of streetlights illuminated the trees growing on Concord's village green. From behind us, inside the inn, came muffled laughter. "He was using me," she said softly. "Using me to get Glen."

"I guess he could've done it without you," I said.

"But I helped."

"For Paul," I said, "I think his relationship with you probably started as a way to get back at Glen. Paul hated the people he defended, hated what they did, hated the fact that they went free, hated himself for every not-guilty verdict he got. Having an affair with you gave him a measure of revenge against Glen."

She was nodding as I spoke. "I guess I was getting some revenge against Glen, too," she said. She laughed quickly. "It's pretty ironic. I was attracted to Glen because he was so weak and dependent and needy. It took me a long time to figure that out, but I did. I thought about leaving him. But I couldn't make myself do it. Because—well, because he was so weak, dependent, and needy. Then Paul Cizek came along, and at first he seemed to be Glen's opposite. He seemed strong and independent and self-sufficient, living out there by himself on Plum Island. But when I got to know him, you know what?"

I nodded.

"Paul turned out to be weak, dependent, and needy, too," she said. "And part of me felt liberated when I heard he drowned. Just the way I feel liberated now that Glen's probably going to die, God help me."

Horowitz called me at my office the next afternoon. "You got some explaining to do, Coyne," he said.

"It's not Paul, is it?"

"No."

"Who is it, then?"

"They haven't figured that out yet. But whoever it is—"

"I know," I said. "Whoever it is, it's Paul Cizek who murdered him."

"Not only that—"

"Right," I said. "His wife was part of it."

"We tried to find her," said Horowitz. "Her Saab is in her garage, but she's not home and she's not at her office."

"She's gone," I said. "And so is Paul."

"We're looking for them," he said. "Now. Explain."

"Here's how I figure it," I said. "After Paul got Glen Falconer off, he separated from his wife and moved to Plum Island, where he began an affair with Glen's wife, and—"

"Whoa," said Horowitz. "What'd you say?"

"Paul was having an affair with Brenda Falconer," I said. "And that gave him the idea of killing Glen. Or maybe he had the idea first, and that's why he began the affair. Either way, he faked his own death and disappeared. He was presumed dead. So no one would suspect him when Glen was run down. When I tracked down Paul, I told him that Eddie Vaccaro was looking for him. That gave him another idea."

"You think Cizek's the one who did Falconer, then?"

"Yes. And Vaccaro, too."

Horowitz paused for a moment. "Pretty good," he said. "He kills a few people. One of 'em he dresses up in his own clothes, and he arranges for his wife to ID the body—"

"He had to," I said. "Because the first time he tried to fake his own death, I tracked him down. This time he made sure I was there to see firsthand that he was dead."

198

"And you bought it," he said.

"Yes," I said. "I did. But I never really looked at him. All I could think of was that whoever blasted Paul could still be lurking around, and we should get the hell out of there and call the police. And Olivia . . . "

"Sure," he said. "She reacted like it was him. And then she ID'd him for the cops. Who'd think to doubt the bereaved wife?"

"Exactly," I said. "Especially if the family lawyer is there to more or less corroborate it. Hell, he was there at the cottage, where we expected to find him. According to Olivia, he'd called saying he was scared, needed help, come fast. In the dark it looked enough like Paul. Dressed like him, same size, lying there on his belly in all that blood . . . "

"Don't beat up on yourself," said Horowitz. "They fooled the cops, too."

"Paul put his ring and watch on the guy," I said. "That was to make Olivia's ID work. And he dressed him in his clothes before he shot him. That was for my benefit. Those New Hampshire police probably never laid eyes on the real Paul Cizek. It wouldn't matter if they eventually realized they'd made a mistake. The Cizeks would be long gone by then."

"As it appears they are," said Horowitz with a sigh. "How'd you figure this out?"

"I didn't exactly figure it out," I said. "Not really. But there were things that didn't fit. Like Thomas Gall, the obvious suspect. I bumped into him once. He was upset, all right. He hit me. But I ended up feeling sorry for the guy. He just didn't seem like a vicious killer. And it turns out that Gall and Cizek had gotten together a couple of times on Plum Island, had a beer. A neighbor of Paul's overheard them talking. It sounded like the two of them were scheming something. I figure Paul told Gall that he was going to take care of Glen Falconer. Glen would be the one Gall hated the most, so that'd satisfy him. He wouldn't need to kill Paul to get the vengeance he wanted."

"So if it wasn't Gall . . . "

"I thought of Eddie Vaccaro, of course," I said. "Turns out he died before Cizek. And that raised the question of who killed Vaccaro. Russo, logically. Except I know for a fact that Russo was still looking for Vaccaro around the time the ME says he was already dead. So not only did Vaccaro not kill Paul Cizek, but . . . "

"I getcha," said Horowitz.

"I was thinking of Olivia, too," I continued. "You always suspect the spouse, and people fool you, but Olivia loved Paul. I'm sure of that. Even if she knew he was shacking up with Brenda Falconer, I couldn't see her as a killer. Anyway, I thought, if it wasn't any of them, who could it be? Which led me to conclude that it wasn't anybody. Paul's not dead. He's not a murder victim at all. On the contrary."

"In which case," said Horowitz, "that body belongs to somebody else. Which is where this conversation started. And the question is, who?"

"Like I told you," I said, "I don't know. But I'd check the whereabouts of some of Paul Cizek's old clients."

"Victor Benton," Horowitz told me on the phone the next morning. "Turns out he's been missing since Monday. The fingerprints matched."

"Victor Benton," I repeated. "The day-care guy who Paul Cizek defended."

"Child molester, kiddie porn. A vile son of a bitch. Nobody thought Cizek could get him off. But he did."

"And then he killed him," I said. "He killed Eddie Vaccaro, too. Paul was doing justice. Killing the bad guys, making up for the fact that he'd defended them successfully." I took a breath. "I forgot to mention before. There's an old pickup truck parked beside that cottage in New Hampshire. You should have your forensics guys check it."

"The vehicle that ran down Falconer, you think?"

"I'd be surprised if it's not."

I heard Horowitz chuckle.

"This is funny?" I said.

"Not hardly." I heard him blow a quick breath into the phone. "We found a Chevy station wagon parked in the outdoor lot by the international terminal at Logan. It was registered to Victor Benton."

"That's the car Paul and Olivia used, you think?"

"Sure. He must've convinced Benton to go visit him in New Hampshire, where he murdered him. Then he scooted in Benton's car. You and her went up there and found Benton's body dressed in Cizek's clothes, wearing Cizek's jewelry, established that it was Cizek, and you drove her home, the grieving widow. Then after you left, he came by in Benton's car, picked her up, and they drove to the airport. Thing is, none of the airlines have any record of either of them taking a flight."

"Fake passports, huh?"

"Probably. Or maybe they didn't go overseas at all."

After I got home and out of my office clothes that evening, I called Alex. When she answered the phone, I said, "I've got a story for you."

"Don't, Brady," she said. "Please."

"Don't what?"

"Don't say what you don't mean."

"Okay," I said. "What I mean is, I miss you terribly and I want to fix things. But I do have a story for you."

I heard her sigh. "I had to leave the other night. I just felt . . . I don't know. Like it was never going to work. I'm sorry."

"Love is never having to say—"

She laughed. "I think I'm gonna puke."

"We've got to try to make it work," I said.

"I know." She hesitated. "So do you want me to come over?"

"More than anything."

"Shall I bring some lentil soup?"

"I love lentil soup."

"Brady—"

"Okay. I'll say what I mean. I don't particularly like lentil soup. But I love you."

"Do you really have a story for me?"

"I've got a story, all right."

27

Brenda Falconer called me on the last Wednesday in July to tell me that Glen had finally died. "His organs were shutting down, one by one," she told me. "Roger and I had already pretty much agreed that he should be taken off life-support. Yesterday his heart stopped and they couldn't get it started again."

"I'm sorry" was all I could think of to say.

Alex and I attended the memorial service at Ste. Anne's Episcopal church in Lincoln on the following Saturday. It was a small, private gathering. I saw none of Roger's old political or business cronies. We sang "A Mighty Fortress Is Our God" and "Onward Christian Soldiers," and the priest read some Scripture and gave a short homily on the subject of dying young and unexpectedly.

There were no eulogies for Glen.

Roger and Brenda sat alone in the front pew, and when the service ended, Roger leaned heavily on her as she helped him up the aisle. In the month or so since I'd last seen him, Roger appeared to have aged twenty years.

Alex and I met them outside. Brenda caught my eye. She lifted her eyebrows, a question and a request, and I nodded. I saw no purpose in mentioning Paul Cizek's name.

Roger's eyes were red and watery, and from the way he mumbled I suspected that he was taking tranquilizers. I didn't mention the fact that the police had examined the pickup truck beside Paul Cizek's cottage in New Hampshire and found traces of paint that matched the bicycle Glen had been riding when he was hit. I didn't know if the police had talked with him about it. If they hadn't, it certainly wasn't up to me.

Brenda said she was going to stay on in the big house in Lincoln to look after Roger, at least for awhile. If she saw that as penance for what she might've perceived as her sins, it was understandable. She'd told me she was attracted to weak, needy, and dependent men. Roger now appeared to qualify admirably.

I reminded her that Glen's estate would need settling. I told her to call the office within the next couple of weeks and we'd get going on it.

While Brenda and I talked, Roger leaned on her arm and stared at the ground. Once in awhile he looked up at her and nodded vacantly. She called him "Roger" with what appeared to be genuine affection, and he called her "dear," and it occurred to me that at least one good thing had resulted from Glen's death.

There was no return address on the envelope, but it was postmarked from Key West. I sat at my kitchen table and tore it open. At the top of the first page of the letter, Olivia Cizek had written, "Somewhere in Florida, sometime in August." Her handwriting was small and precise.

> Dear Brady,
>
> An explanation is overdue, I know. Or an apology. I lied to a lot of people. But lying to you was the worst. You were very kind to me.
>
> I'm feeling guilty enough. But I want you to know that I had nothing to do with what Paul did, right up to that night when we went to his place in New Hampshire. He did not tell me he was going to fake his death on his boat. He certainly didn't tell me he planned to murder three men.

When he called that night, I thought he was a ghost. I guess I was so stunned I would have agreed to do anything. He made it sound simple. There would be a dead man at his cottage. You, dear Brady, knew how to get there. All I had to do was get you to take me up there. I'd say the body was Paul. After that we'd be together again.

It didn't seem wrong when he explained it. I didn't ask any questions. Like I said, I was so surprised and dazed I couldn't really think. I just called you, and you know what happened after that.

You must think I'm quite a liar, or a great actress. I'm not. Not really. All the emotions I felt that night were real. The whole thing was crazy. I guess *I* was a little crazy—first hearing Paul's voice, then hearing his plan, and then, dear God, seeing that body. I was in a daze the whole night. The lies just came out the way Paul had given them to me.

I knew he'd gone over the edge, of course. But I denied it to myself. And even after it was over, I kept trying to deny it. He killed evil men. That's what he said. They deserved to die, to pay for their crimes, and I tried to convince myself that it was okay, that he had made justice happen.

But it didn't work. I know what he did—and what I helped him to do—is wrong. I'm glad I know that. It means I'm not crazy.

I knew he was having an affair with somebody, although I tried to deny it. He told me it was with the wife of that drunken driver he defended. He saw it as a kind of revenge, or retribution, as if that made it okay. I can forgive the affair. But I can't forgive him for doing it out of malice instead of love.

Anyway, Brady, now I've left him. I don't know where he is. Wandering around the Caribbean in his sailboat, I guess. He's a man without a country and without a family and without a career, and even though I know he's done horrible things, I feel sorry for him. But I can't be with him.

I'm staying with friends for now. They know everything. I'm afraid they'll get in trouble if I'm found here, so I guess I'll have to move on pretty soon. Some day I know I'll have to face up to my part of it. I won't be able to live this way much longer. I'll need a lawyer, so you can expect to hear from me again.

But I'm not quite ready. Not yet.

I hope you can forgive me.

She had signed it, "Very fondly, Olivia."

I called Horowitz, and he came by my office the following afternoon to pick up Olivia's letter. He read it, smiled, and said, "Oh, well."

"Now what happens?" I said.

"Oh, I'll turn this over to the feds. We'll see."

"He could get away with it?"

"He's roaming around the Caribbean on a sailboat? I guess he could."

"What about Olivia?"

"Everyone'd like to get her story. Be good if she'd turn herself in. She might not even be prosecuted. Not under the circumstances. It wouldn't take a Paul Cizek to get a jury crying over her story. Hell, even you could get her off."

"Thanks, pal," I said. I shook my head. "It's not right, though. Paul murdered three men. And he betrayed a lot of others."

"Like you."

"Yes," I said. "Like me."

Horowitz shrugged. "The feds've got their priorities. Nobody's exactly clamoring for blood in this case. I'd guess that unless Cizek does something stupid, sooner or later everybody'll forget about it. Nobody's mourning the deaths of a hit man, a child molester, and a drunk driver."

"Doesn't that piss you off?"

206

"It doesn't matter if it pisses me off, Coyne. That's the thing that guys like Cizek need to remember. Do the job. That's all. Feelings just get in the way." He jabbed my shoulder with his forefinger. "You too. You should remember that."

I nodded. "I guess you're right."

At 8:00 A.M. on the day before Labor Day, Joey and a gang of his old high-school friends backed a rented Ryder truck up to Alex's Marlborough Street apartment. They had her stuff loaded onto the truck by eleven, and by six that afternoon it had all been unloaded into her new place in Garrison, Maine.

We ate takeout pizza and drank sodas on Alex's deck, and then the boys piled into the truck and headed back for Boston.

Alex and I lingered on the deck. We sipped the housewarming champagne I'd brought and propped our heels up on the railing and watched the color fade from the western sky.

"Your balcony faces east," she said quietly. "You can watch the sun come up. My deck faces west. I see it set. What do you make of that?"

"It's probably profoundly significant," I said. "But damned if I know why."

"One of these days," she said a minute or two later, "we're going to have to figure it out."

"The significance of east and west?"

"No. What we're gonna do."

I reached for her hand. "I can't just chuck it all," I said.

She gave my hand a squeeze.

"I've got my clients, my friends, my routines. It's usually not stimulating. But it's my life."

"I understand," she murmured.

"And once in a while I get a—a case. Like Paul Cizek. And it's stimulating as hell."

"That's okay, Brady," said Alex.

I turned to face her. "I didn't want to tell you until I'd worked it out," I said. "I'll be closing my office on Fridays, beginning in October. It'll mean working a little harder the rest of the week, at least for awhile. But most of the time I should be able to drive up on Thursday evenings. It's only two and a half hours."

"So we'll have long weekends together?"

"Things might come up," I said. "But, yes. That's my goal. Thursday night through Sunday. If that's okay."

"And if I have to write in the mornings sometimes, that's okay with you?"

"There are lots of streams and ponds around here to explore," I said, "and you'll have firewood that needs splitting and various domestic chores that will require the attention of a handy person such as I. I'll try to stay out of your way."

"It's not exactly starting over again in Montana," she murmured.

"Maybe some people can do this sort of thing all at once," I said. "Paul Cizek tried. He couldn't make it work. Even Thoreau, when he lived at Walden, kept going home to visit his mother in Concord. I just don't think it's that easy, leaving everything behind. Anyway, I know me. I have to feel my way along."

She leaned toward me and kissed me under the ear. "So how does it feel so far?" she whispered.

"It feels like a commitment," I said.

"Scary, huh?"

"No," I said. "Actually, it feels just right."